The Compass of the Moon and Stars

Authors Name : Ian Mcewan
Published in 2024

TABLE OF CONTENT

Chapter 1: The Village of Roslyn   1

Chapter 2: The Order of the Hidden Compass   4

Chapter 3: The Mysterious Package   7

Chapter 4: The Druid's Secret   13

Chapter 5: The Secrets Beneath   17

Chapter 6: The Passage of Trials   21

Chapter 7: The Guardians of the Henge   25

Chapter 8: The Starry Night Revelation   36

Chapter 9: The Druids Legacy   40

Chapter 10: The Choice   46

Chapter 11: The Return Home   51

Chapter 12: The Disturbance   53

Chapter 13: The Hiding Place   55

Chapter 14: Epilogue - The Adventure Continues   58

Published by:
Independently published
United Kingdom

The Compass of the Moon and Stars

Chapter 1: The Village of Rosslyn

The small village of Rosslyn, nestled in the rolling hills just outside Edinburgh, held a timeless charm, as though it had been forgotten by the modern world. Its cobblestone streets wound lazily between clusters of cottages, their slanted roofs covered with moss and ivy that clung to the stone walls like creeping memories of the past. The air was always fresh, carrying the earthy scent of rain-soaked leaves and wood smoke from the chimneys that puffed faint trails of smoke into the sky. It was the kind of place where life moved at a slower pace, where old traditions lingered, and the past seemed to whisper from every corner.

At the heart of the village stood Rosslyn Chapel, a place of ancient reverence and mystery. Its stone walls, weathered by centuries, were adorned with the most intricate carvings—patterns and symbols that seemed to hold secrets from a time long forgotten. The chapel had always been a source of fascination for Max and Lottie, ever since they were young. But lately, it had taken on a heavier weight in their hearts, its history mingling with their own.

Max and Lottie now lived with their grandfather, Grandpa Ben, after the terrible accident that had taken their parents' lives. It had been a cold winter night, the roads slick with ice when tragedy struck. That night seemed like a blur now—a night of flashing lights, the sounds of sirens, and the bitter cold that seeped into their bones. But the ache of loss remained, hovering over their new lives like a shadow that refused to lift.

For Max, the change had been jarring. Once, his days had been filled with laughter and light, his mind occupied with the kinds of carefree thoughts that only come with childhood. But now, his world felt quieter, as if something vital had been taken away. The nights were the hardest. He would lie in bed, staring at

the ceiling, and listen to the silence of the house, his mind filled with echoes of things unsaid. Words he wished he could have spoken to his parents, moments he wished he could have shared with them.

Lottie, though younger, carried the sadness in her own way. She had clung to Grandpa Ben with a fierceness Max had never seen before, as though she were afraid that if she let go, she might lose him too. At times, she seemed like her old self, with her playful smiles and curious nature, but there was a depth to her now, a quietness that hadn't been there before. She had grown up too quickly, forced to face a world where things didn't always end happily.

Though they had both adapted to their new life with Grandpa Ben, nothing could fill the void left behind by their parents. The cottage they now called home was small and cozy, filled with the smell of herbs and the musty scent of old books that Grandpa Ben kept scattered throughout the house. The walls were lined with shelves overflowing with texts on history, myth, and the natural world, a reflection of Grandpa Ben's own lifelong curiosity. But even with the warmth of the hearth and the comfort of their grandfather's stories, there was an emptiness that neither Max nor Lottie could shake.

Yet, despite the sadness that clung to them, Max and Lottie had a way of escaping. They filled their days by dreaming up adventures, letting their imaginations carry them to distant lands where anything was possible. The forest that surrounded Rosslyn Chapel became their haven, a place where they could forget the real world and lose themselves in the wild. The dense trees, tall and ancient, whispered in the wind, and the sound of their laughter would echo through the woods as they ran, pretending to be explorers or knights on a quest, their hearts full of the stories they created.

In the shadow of the trees, they became whoever they wanted to be—brave adventurers, treasure hunters, even heroes saving the world from ancient evils. They would crouch low, pretending to search for hidden relics beneath the roots of the great oaks, or climb the hills to get a better view of their imaginary kingdoms. Every nook and cranny of the forest became part of their story, every stream a boundary to be crossed, every rock a hidden artifact to be uncovered.

The chapel itself, with its ancient stone carvings and air of mystery, was another source of endless inspiration. Max often stood in awe of the intricate work inside, his fingers tracing the lines of the stone figures, dragons and angels, mythical creatures and cryptic symbols. He would marvel at the skill it must have taken to create something so detailed, so precise. "The apprentices who worked here must have been incredible," Max would say, his voice full of wonder. Lottie always nodded in agreement, her wide eyes soaking in the history that surrounded them.

They often imagined what life must have been like for those who carved the chapel's walls centuries ago. In their minds, the apprentices weren't just builders—they were guardians of ancient secrets, men and women who understood the mysteries of the universe. "Do you think they knew magic?" Lottie would ask, her voice a mix of curiosity and excitement.

"Maybe," Max would reply, grinning. "Maybe they were hiding something even bigger than we know."

The stories Grandpa Ben told them about the chapel only fueled their imaginations further. He spoke of secret societies and hidden meanings, of groups who believed that Rosslyn held the key to ancient knowledge, knowledge that could change the world if it were ever unlocked. Max and Lottie would listen intently, their minds spinning with possibilities. They would explore the grounds of the chapel, pretending to be treasure hunters or spies, searching for clues left behind by ancient civilizations.

Every stone, every shadow seemed to hold a secret, waiting to be discovered. The carvings on the walls became codes to be cracked, the statues became sentinels watching over long-lost relics, and the forest paths led to hidden places where only the bravest could venture. To Max and Lottie, Rosslyn was not just a village—it was a gateway to something bigger, something magical. And though they had lost much, their adventures kept them going, filling the empty spaces in their hearts with stories of danger, heroism, and hope.

Chapter 2: The Order of the Hidden Compass

Edinburgh, with its towering castle perched on the craggy cliffs and its winding cobblestone streets, had always been a city of secrets. Beneath its historical charm and tourist-filled alleys lay an unseen Edinburgh—one woven with shadows and stories that most people would never hear. Beneath the grand facades of Georgian townhouses, hidden beneath the layers of history, whispers of ancient orders, clandestine societies, and unseen forces quietly shaped the course of the city's existence. And one of the oldest secrets was "The Order of the Hidden Compass," a group so deeply buried in the folds of time that even those who thought they knew Edinburgh's hidden history would never have heard of it.

To the untrained eye, Edinburgh was a city of festivals, bustling with modernity and culture. Tourists wandered the Royal Mile, snapping photos of the grandiose castle, sipping coffee in small cafés, unaware of the layers of mystery that lurked beneath their feet. But Alastair MacKinnon knew better. The city had many faces—one for the world, and one for those who knew where to look.

Alastair had lived in Edinburgh his entire life, growing up among the narrow streets and stone buildings of the Old Town. From his small flat, tucked away in a shadowy corner of the city, he had watched Edinburgh change over the years, watched it grow and modernize. Yet, through all that change, the city's mysteries remained constant. And through it all, Alastair had remained vigilant—a quiet observer, watching for signs of trouble that most would never notice.

He wasn't a man of renown or importance in the eyes of the world, nor did he seek to be. His life was one of quiet routine, spent running a small antique shop near Grass-market, a place filled with old books, trinkets, and relics of the past. Tourists wandered in, marveling at the dusty artifacts and weathered tomes, never knowing that among the shelves and display cases were objects of far greater importance—artifacts connected to a secret order whose roots stretched back long before Edinburgh was ever built.

The Order of the Hidden Compass had been Alastair's responsibility for most of

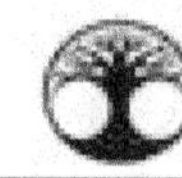

his life, a duty passed down through generations of his family. His father before him, and his father's father, had been part of the order's intricate web, serving as protectors of knowledge far too dangerous to be left in the hands of the unprepared. As a boy, Alastair had been taught the order's ways, sworn to secrecy and bound to its purpose.

The order's history was ancient, older than the city itself. It had been founded long before recorded history, during a time when the world was governed by forces few understood. Its members were not kings or lords, but guardians, protectors of relics that held immense power—relics that could alter the course of history if they fell into the wrong hands. The compass was one of those relics, an object said to hold the key to unlocking the ancient wisdom of the druids and connecting the present to a distant past.

Alastair had served the order faithfully, though his role was not one of action but of observation. The order rarely contacted him directly anymore. His life had become a quiet one, watching from the shadows, ensuring that the secrets he protected remained hidden. His antique shop served as a front, a place where he could quietly keep an eye on the world around him, waiting for signs of trouble. And though the world had changed, Alastair's duty had not.

The last time the order had contacted him, it had been decades ago. Their methods were always the same—no phone calls, no emails, nothing that could be traced. Instead, messages were delivered through coded letters or inconspicuous couriers, their messages shrouded in secrecy. The order had once been a constant presence in his life, but as the years passed, their communications had dwindled. Alastair had begun to think that the world no longer needed such protections, that the relics and the dangers they posed had been forgotten by time.

But everything changed one cold evening.

It had been a normal day in the shop, quiet and uneventful. The tourists had come and gone, leaving behind the scent of damp coats and curiosity. As dusk began to settle over the city, Alastair prepared to close up, locking the display cases and tidying the shelves. That's when he saw it—a small, unmarked parcel sitting on his doorstep.

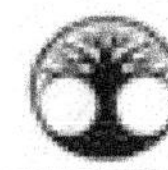

The package was unassuming, wrapped in plain brown paper, but as soon as Alastair picked it up, he knew. His heart raced in his chest, a mixture of dread and anticipation creeping into his veins. The parcel bore the mark of the order, though subtle—their seal, a simple compass etched into wax. He hadn't received anything from the order in years. Why now?

He carried the package to the back of the shop, his fingers trembling slightly as he unwrapped the paper. Inside was an intricately carved wooden box. He opened it carefully, revealing a letter tucked inside, written in the cryptic language of the order. It had been a long time since he had deciphered one of these, but the symbols came back to him easily, like old friends greeting him after a long absence.

The letter was brief, but its message was clear: the order had a new mission for him. After years of silence, they needed him to deliver something—an artifact of great importance—to a boy named Max. The letter didn't explain why Max had been chosen, nor what the boy was meant to do, but the instructions were precise: the compass had chosen its next bearer, and it was Alastair's responsibility to ensure it reached him safely.

Alastair's breath caught in his throat as he lifted the velvet lining of the box to reveal the compass. It was the same one his family had sworn to protect, passed down through the centuries. Its polished wooden surface was smooth from the touch of countless hands, and the needle glowed faintly in the dim light, as though it were alive—vibrating with a hidden energy.

He had heard the stories of the compass, the legends that surrounded it, but he had never truly believed he would be the one to pass it on. That task, he had always thought, would fall to someone else. But now, the weight of history sat in his hands, heavy and unavoidable.

The letter warned of danger, though it did not specify from where. The order's enemies had always been elusive, lurking in the shadows, waiting for the chance to strike. Alastair knew that delivering the compass would not be a simple task. It required secrecy, precision, and, above all, trust. Trust that the boy, Max, was ready for the burden that came with the compass. Trust that Alastair himself was

still capable of fulfilling his duty.

As he sat at his desk, the compass in his hands, Alastair felt the weight of his mission pressing down on him. He had grown old in the service of the order, and yet, he had never truly questioned its purpose until now. Why Max? What had the order seen in him? Why had they waited so long to pass on the compass?

There were no answers in the letter, only the command: deliver the compass, and ensure it reaches its intended bearer. As always, the order worked in shadows, leaving Alastair with little more than his instincts to guide him.

With a sigh, Alastair stood and locked the shop for the night, tucking the compass into the inner pocket of his coat. The journey ahead would take him deep into the heart of Edinburgh, but more than that, it would carry him into the unknown—a path that had been set long before his time. The order's work was never truly finished, and now, after all these years, it had come back to him.

The compass had chosen Max, and whether the boy was ready or not, his adventure was about to begin

Chapter 3: The Mysterious Package

Max lay sprawled on his bed, staring up at the ceiling, his mind drifting aimlessly as the lazy afternoon sunbathed the village in warmth. The small village of Rosslyn, nestled just outside Edinburgh, was usually a haven of peace, its winding cobblestone streets and rolling hillsides the perfect backdrop for lazy summer days. Max loved the quiet charm of the village, the way the tall trees rustled with the slightest breeze, and how Rosslyn Chapel, the village's famous medieval church, stood tall and proud on its ancient foundation, watching over everything like a silent guardian.

Rosslyn Chapel had always fascinated Max. It wasn't just its breathtaking architecture or the incredible carvings that seemed to tell stories older than time

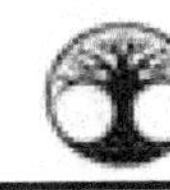

itself. No, it was the mystery that surrounded the place. People whispered about secret societies, hidden treasures, and ancient knowledge. Over the centuries, the chapel had drawn historians, conspiracy theorists, and adventurers alike, all seeking the truth behind its stone walls. Max and Lottie had grown up exploring the chapel grounds, their imaginations running wild with tales of knights, secret orders, and ancient relics. Little did they know, those stories were closer to the truth than they realized.

Today, though, even the mysteries of the chapel couldn't shake the feeling of boredom that clung to Max. The summer sun blazed down, casting the village outside in a warm, golden haze, but inside his room, where the curtains were drawn tight, the air felt thick and stale, as if it had given up trying to move.

Below him, Lottie sat on the floor, her toy soldiers marching in orderly rows, their plastic boots clicking softly against the carpet. The rhythmic sound was almost hypnotic, though Max barely noticed, his mind drifting to how little had happened this summer.

"Bored?" Lottie asked, not bothering to look up, her voice casual, but with an edge of knowing that only siblings could master.

"Terribly," Max groaned, his arms flopping uselessly at his sides. "It feels like this whole summer's just... stuck. Like nothing's ever going to happen."

As if the universe had been waiting for those very words, the doorbell rang. The chime echoed through the quiet house, slicing through the heavy air like a blade. Max and Lottie exchanged glances; their boredom instantly replaced by a flicker of curiosity. They were not expecting anyone.

"Race you!" Lottie shouted, already springing up from the floor. Max scrambled after her, heart racing—finally, something different. But Lottie, faster as always, flung open the door with a triumphant grin.

Standing on the doorstep was a man unlike anyone they had ever seen before. He was tall and thin, his figure all harsh angles beneath a faded brown coat. His long, pointy nose twitched when he smiled—a smile that seemed more like a grimace, never reaching his sharp, dark eyes. His bushy mustache, nearly too large

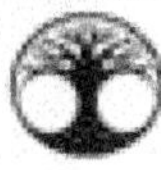

for his narrow face, quivered slightly as he spoke.

"Delivery for Master Max and Miss Lottie," he rasped, his voice dry and gravelly, like leaves being crunched underfoot in the dead of autumn.

As the delivery man stood on Max and Lottie's doorstep, he couldn't help but feel a weight in his chest—one that he had carried for years. He watched the children with a sense of familiarity, though they wouldn't know him. How could they? He had spent most of his life in the shadows, just like every member of the secret order.

It had been nearly thirty years since he had joined them, though the memories were still sharp, as if they had just happened yesterday. He remembered the day clearly—the day he took the oath. He had been young then, eager to understand the mysteries of the world. The allure of the order, the promise of knowledge that stretched back farther than the pyramids, had been irresistible. He hadn't known then just how heavy the burden of those secrets would be.

The Order of the Hidden Compass had been established long before recorded history, a time when the world was governed by forces and knowledge that most would never comprehend. Its purpose was simple yet profound: to unite and protect the heritage of an ancient race, a lineage whose roots stretched far beyond the reaches of modern civilization. They were the keepers of forgotten lore, of relics that could reshape the world if they fell into the wrong hands. Each member, upon initiation, swore a vow of secrecy, a vow that bound them for life. The delivery man had taken that vow, never once questioning it.

Over the years, he had seen many faces come and go, each one carrying the same haunted look after their initiation. The order's work was silent, invisible to the world at large, but crucial. For decades, he had served, delivering ancient artefact's to chosen individuals, ensuring that the order's secrets remained protected, hidden away from those who would misuse them.

As he handed over the small package, his mind wandered to the day he was first entrusted with such a delivery. He had been nervous then, his hands shaking as

he carried an artifact whose significance he couldn't even comprehend. Now, it was second nature. Yet, this particular delivery felt different. There was something in the air, a heaviness that clung to him, as if the weight of time itself had wrapped around this small, unassuming package.

He tipped his hat to the children, a subtle nod that held more meaning than they could possibly understand. With quick, deliberate steps, he walked away, disappearing around the corner as swiftly as he had appeared. His task was complete, but the order's work was far from over. The compass had chosen them, and now, their journey was just beginning.

Max hesitated as he reached out to take the package. The string was knotted in an intricate, almost impossible pattern, and the box, though small, felt heavier than it should have—as if something more than just its contents weighed it down.

Max opened his mouth to ask the man something—Who are you? Where's this from? —but before he could speak, the man had already turned, striding away with quick, deliberate steps. Max blinked, watching as the man disappeared around the corner of the hedge—too quickly, almost as if he'd melted into the shadows themselves. A strange unease curled in Max's stomach, like a cold, creeping sensation brushing the inside of his skin.

"Who was that?" Max asked, more to himself than Lottie, his voice barely a murmur.

Lottie shrugged, more interested in the mysterious package than the man who had delivered it. "Who cares!" Lottie's eyes were already locked on the box, her curiosity overcoming anything else. She dragged the box inside, and Max followed, the weight of it strangely pressing in his hands, the rough paper crackling beneath his fingers.

They placed it on the living room table. The dim light filtering through the curtains caught the strange carvings beneath the wrapping paper, making them glimmer faintly, almost as if they shifted when you weren't looking. Lottie leaned in closer, her breath catching in her throat, and Max noticed the slight tremor in

her hand as she reached out.

"What do you think it is?" she whispered, her earlier confidence faltering just a little.

Max hesitated. The carvings looked ancient, their intricate lines seeming to pulse with some hidden energy. His heart thudded in his chest, a strange mixture of excitement and dread tangling together. Slowly, almost cautiously, he tugged at the knotted string. It resisted at first, the twine scraping against his skin as if it didn't want to let go, but with a final pull, the knot came free.

Max peeled away the wrapping. Beneath it was an old wooden box, its surface worn smooth by time, but still sturdy. The symbols on the lid were unlike anything Max had ever seen before, etched deep into the wood. They seemed almost to hum—or was that the air itself?

As Max lifted the lid, the world seemed to hold its breath. Inside, nestled on a bed of deep blue velvet, was something that shimmered faintly in the dim light.

"A compass," Lottie breathed, awe creeping into her voice. But not just any compass. Its base was made of dark, polished wood, smooth to the touch, and the face was inlaid with intricate designs of the moon and stars. The needle spun lazily, glowing faintly as it turned, and with each slow circle, the air seemed to shift around them—as though the room itself was breathing.

Max reached out, hesitating as his fingers hovered above it. The compass felt alive, somehow warm beneath his touch, as though it had been waiting for him. When he finally picked it up, the needle stopped spinning. Instantly. It shot upwards, pointing straight at the ceiling, and at that same moment, the moon on the compass face began to glow, casting a soft, silvery light that bathed the room in an ethereal glow. It wasn't warm or cold—it was something else entirely, like the stillness of a winter night, cool yet comforting.

Lottie gasped, her wide eyes fixed on the compass as the tiny stars on its face began to twinkle, their light flickering like fireflies caught in a soft summer breeze. A faint vibration thrummed through the floor, barely noticeable at first, but slowly growing, until Max could feel it in his bones, pulsing like a heartbeat.

Max's own heart pounded in his chest, the excitement battling with something deeper, a quiet, persistent unease that he couldn't shake. He glanced at Lottie, whose face was alight with wonder, completely lost in the moment.

"That's not just any compass," Max whispered, his voice so low it barely broke the thick air. "It's… magic."

Before either of them could say more, soft footsteps shuffled behind them. Max turned, his pulse quickening again, but not from excitement this time. Grandpa Ben stood in the doorway, leaning casually on his walking stick, though Max was certain he didn't need it. His thick silver hair stuck up in wild tufts, and his eyes sparkled with the familiar mischief Max had grown up with, but now, there was something else there too—something serious.

"I see you've found it," Grandpa Ben said, his voice warm, but low. He stepped closer, his gaze lingering on the glowing compass. "It's been waiting for you."

Max swallowed, feeling the weight of the compass grow heavier in his hand. "Grandpa, where did this come from?" Lottie asked, running to hug him, though her eyes never left the glowing object.

Grandpa Ben smiled, but there was something guarded in his expression. "That, my dear, is a very special compass. It once belonged to a druid who lived thousands of years ago. He used it to find the most magical places in the world. And now, it's found its way to you."

Max felt the air grow thicker again, as though the room itself was pressing in on him. "But why does it glow? And why did it stop spinning?" His voice was tight, uncertain.

Grandpa Ben's gaze softened, but there was still that cautious look. "Because," he said quietly, "it's chosen you, Max. The compass points to something important—something hidden. But to discover what that is, you'll have to follow where it leads."

Max and Lottie exchanged a glance, the ordinary summer afternoon now feeling impossibly distant. Excitement buzzed in the air, thick and electric, but Max

couldn't shake that knot of unease.

"Where is it pointing?" Max asked, barely managing to keep his voice steady.

Grandpa Ben's eyes flicked to the compass before meeting Max's. "To a place older than time itself. A place where the secrets of the ancient world are kept. It's pointing to Stonehenge."

Lottie gasped, her excitement bubbling over, but Max felt a cold shiver crawl up his spine. Stonehenge. He'd heard Grandpa talk about it before—whispers of ancient power, of mysteries that had never been solved. Mysteries best left alone, Grandpa had once said.

"But be warned," Grandpa Ben added, his voice low and serious now, his hand resting heavily on Max's shoulder. "This isn't just any adventure. The compass will test you—challenge you. And it will take you to places you've never dreamed of. But if you're brave, and if you trust each other, you might just discover something that has been lost to the world for thousands of years."

Max swallowed hard, the weight of Grandpa's words settling in his chest like stones. He looked at Lottie, who was practically glowing with excitement. She was ready, eager to leap into the unknown.

But Max wasn't so sure. Something about this compass, about where it was leading them, felt bigger than them—older and more dangerous than anything they could imagine. Their ordinary summer had just turned into something else entirely.

An adventure. One Max wasn't sure they were ready for.

Chapter 4: The Druid's Secret

The fire crackled softly in the hearth as Max and Lottie sat on the edge of their seats, their eyes locked on their grandfather. Outside, the wind howled, rattling

the windows of the old house, but inside, the room felt warm, safe, and filled with anticipation. Shadows danced across the walls, cast by the flickering flames, giving the room a feeling of both comfort and mystery. Grandpa Ben leaned back in his worn leather chair, his face lit by the orange glow of the fire, his eyes glinting with a deep, secret knowledge that he had carried for years. It was a look Max and Lottie had come to recognize—a look that meant he was about to tell a story worth remembering.

"All right, all right," Grandpa Ben said, chuckling at their impatience. He loved these moments, when his grandchildren hung on every word. "You want to know about the druids? Well, I'll tell you, but I warn you, not everything is as it seems. The druids were more than just men who worshiped trees and stars, oh no. They were the keepers of something far more powerful."

Max and Lottie leaned in closer, their faces illuminated by the firelight, their imaginations already racing. The sound of the wind outside seemed to fade as they became completely absorbed in their grandfather's words.

"The druids," Grandpa Ben began, his voice soft and low, "were a mysterious group. They were deeply connected to the forces of nature and the universe itself. They believed that everything in the world—every tree, every river, every star in the sky—was part of a grand, interconnected web of magic. And they knew how to tap into that magic, to use it to heal, to guide, and to protect. But they didn't just use it for themselves. No, they were far too wise for that. They were protectors of ancient knowledge, knowledge that could shape the fate of the world."

He paused, letting the weight of his words sink in. Max and Lottie exchanged glances, their curiosity and excitement only growing with each moment. The fire crackled louder, as if it, too, were hanging on Grandpa Ben's every word.

"But there's something most people don't know about them," Grandpa Ben continued, his voice dropping to a near whisper, drawing Max and Lottie even closer. "It wasn't just nature they were connected to—it was the stars. The druids had an ancient understanding of the cosmos, far greater than most people give them credit for. They believed that the stars were more than just distant lights.

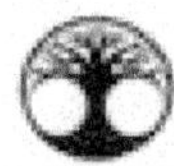

To them, the stars were guides, messengers from beyond our world. The druids could read the stars like we read books, and they believed that the constellations held the answers to questions mankind hadn't even thought to ask yet."

Lottie's eyes widened with wonder. "You mean, like astrology? Did they predict the future?"

"In a way, yes," Grandpa Ben said, nodding. "But their understanding went beyond mere predictions. The druids didn't just read the stars for omens or prophecies. They believed the stars were connected to places on Earth—sacred places, where the energy of the universe was strongest. And at these places, the veil between our world and the next was thin. Stonehenge, for example."

Max sat up straighter at the mention of Stonehenge, the thrill of the mystery bubbling up inside him. "Stonehenge?" he asked, his voice filled with excitement.

Grandpa Ben nodded again, his face serious but alive with the telling. "Yes, Stonehenge wasn't just a monument. It was a gateway. A place where the energy of the earth and the sky connected. The druids built it with purpose, aligning the stones with the stars to harness that power. They didn't build it as a place for rituals or sacrifices—that's just what the history books want you to think. No, Stonehenge was built to protect something ancient, something so powerful that it could change the world if it were ever unlocked."

Lottie's brow furrowed, the questions tumbling out of her. "What were they protecting, Grandpa?"

Grandpa Ben's smile faded slightly, and for the first time, Max and Lottie could see the seriousness in his eyes. "They called it the Heart of the Sky," he said quietly. "No one knows exactly what it was, or what it could do, but the druids believed it was a source of unimaginable power. Some say it was a relic from before mankind even walked the earth, a key to unlocking the mysteries of the universe. Others believe it was a gift from the stars themselves, a way to communicate with forces beyond our understanding."

The firelight flickered as if in response to Grandpa Ben's words, casting eerie shadows across the room. Max and Lottie were completely enthralled now, their

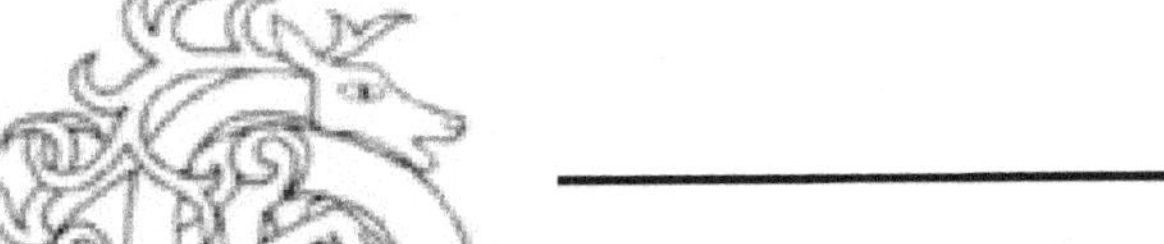

imaginations running wild with images of ancient relics and cosmic forces.

Grandpa Ben leaned forward, lowering his voice to just above a whisper, his face serious. "But the druids didn't just guard the Heart of the Sky. They hid it. They knew the power it held could be dangerous in the wrong hands. And so, they scattered clues about its location, leaving only a select few trusted individuals to guard its secret. That's why they were so connected to nature and the stars—because those were the only things that could guide someone to the heart."

Max felt a chill run down his spine. The idea of ancient secrets hidden beneath the stars and the earth was both thrilling and terrifying. His mind raced with questions, but one rose above the rest. "Do you think the compass... our compass... has anything to do with it?"

Grandpa Ben's eyes twinkled with a secret, but he didn't answer right away. "Ah, the compass," he said, his voice thoughtful. "That's a story for another time. But you're not far off, Max. The compass, much like the stars, points the way to something important—something hidden."

Lottie, her curiosity burning, leaned in even closer. "So, do you think we'll find it, Grandpa? The Heart of the Sky?"

Grandpa Ben chuckled softly, though his eyes remained serious. "I can't say for sure," he said slowly. "But Stonehenge has always been more than it seems. If you're going there, you'll be stepping into a place where the very fabric of time and space is thinner than anywhere else. The druids knew this. They used the stars and the stones to align with forces we can only imagine."

The room fell silent for a moment, the weight of Grandpa Ben's words settling over them. Outside, the wind howled once more, but inside, Max and Lottie were filled with a heady mixture of excitement and fear.

"Whatever happens," Grandpa Ben said softly, his voice full of wisdom and love, "remember this: the druids believed that those who were brave, wise, and true would always find their way. Trust in the compass, trust in yourselves, and who knows what you might uncover."

Max and Lottie exchanged a determined look, their nerves now tingling with anticipation. They didn't know what Stonehenge had in store for them, but one thing was certain—whatever secrets the ancient site held, they were ready to face them together.

Chapter 5: The Secrets Beneath

The journey from Edinburgh to Stonehenge had been long and winding, filled with quiet moments where Zara, Max, Lottie, and Grandpa Ben were left alone with their thoughts. Leaving behind the quaint village of Rosslyn and the ever-mysterious Rosslyn Chapel, they had boarded a train south, watching the Scottish hills give way to the flat expanses of England. As they traveled, the weight of their mission grew heavier, and even the beauty of the passing countryside couldn't lighten the strange sense of anticipation they all felt.

Max had spent much of the journey staring out of the window, his mind still reeling from everything that had happened. The compass, the strange carvings, and now their sudden trek to one of the world's most famous monuments—it all felt too surreal. Lottie, on the other hand, had been unusually quiet. She clutched a small notebook, jotting down thoughts and sketches of what she imagined they would find at Stonehenge. Zara had spent the trip turning the compass over in her hands, feeling its warmth and the faint vibration that had never ceased since they had left their village.

Grandpa Ben sat in contemplative silence, his eyes closed for most of the ride, as if reliving memories only he could understand. Though the others didn't ask, Zara could tell he knew far more about what they were walking into than he let on. His connection to both Rosslyn Chapel and Stonehenge seemed deeper than any of them realized, and Zara knew, instinctively, that this was more than just a family story. There were layers to Grandpa Ben's past—layers tied to the compass and the mysteries that lay ahead.

When they arrived in Wiltshire, the sky had begun to darken. As they approached

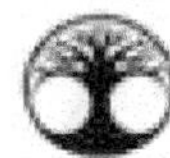

Stonehenge by car, the great monument loomed in the distance, a silhouette against the dimming sky. The sight of the ancient stones standing tall, casting their long shadows across the open plain, sent a shiver through Zara. It wasn't just the sight of them—it was what they represented. A mystery as old as time itself.

The air around Stonehenge was different from anywhere else. It was as if the very atmosphere hummed with energy, a force that had been harnessed by those who had once built this place. The temperature dropped as the sun began to set, and a chill crept into the air, making Zara clutch her jacket tighter around her shoulders.

The four of them stood before the towering stones, their eyes scanning the ancient monument that had stood for millennial. In Zara's hand, the magical compass trembled, its needle spinning wildly, as if urging them forward.

Grandpa Ben, their trusted guide, stared at the stones with an intensity that made the others glance at him with curiosity. His usual easy-going manner had shifted into something more focused, almost reverent. How did he know so much?

Zara, always the most inquisitive, couldn't hold back her curiosity any longer. "Grandpa, how do you know so much about this place? It's like... you've been here before."

Grandpa Ben smiled, though a shadow passed across his face. "I have my reasons, Zara. Let's just say our family has a connection to this place." He paused, his eyes distant. "My own grandfather used to tell stories—stories about a time when druids walked these lands, wielding powers we can barely comprehend today. And that compass you're holding," he nodded toward it, "has been in our family for generations. It's always pointed somewhere, though we never knew why. Until now."

Max and Lottie exchanged a look, their interest piqued, but there was an unspoken concern between them. Grandpa Ben wasn't telling them everything.

They moved closer to the stones, their footsteps soft against the grass. The mon-

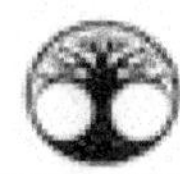

ument felt alive in a way that defied logic. The towering stones—massive slabs of rock—stood in perfect alignment, as though placed there with purpose beyond mere construction. The alignment of Stonehenge with the sun during the solstices had always intrigued historians, but Grandpa Ben's stories made it clear that the druids had built this place for more than just stargazing. They believed in the energy of the earth itself, energy they could harness and channel, and Stonehenge was the key.

Zara ran her fingers over the rough surface of one of the larger stones and noticed a spiral symbol carved into it, barely visible under layers of weather and time. As she traced it with her finger, a strange warmth spread through her hand. A shiver ran down her spine. "What's this symbol?"

Grandpa Ben's face darkened. His voice lowered. "The spiral is ancient—older than Stonehenge itself, perhaps. The druids believed it represented the cycles of life, the connection between the material and spiritual worlds. But here… in the context of Stonehenge, it's something more." He hesitated, his eyes narrowing. "Some say it marks places of power, where the earth's energy can be harnessed. But it's not meant for just anyone to use."

Lottie stepped closer; her voice edged with unease. "Why not?"

Grandpa Ben's gaze flicked to the stones, and his expression grew even graver. "Because the energy here is unpredictable. Dangerous. There are forces in this place that don't want us to succeed." He glanced around as if expecting to see something lurking just out of sight.

The words hung heavy in the air. Max shifted nervously, glancing over his shoulder. "Do you think we're being watched?" he asked, his voice barely more than a whisper.

Before anyone could answer, a sudden gust of wind whipped through the stones, colder than the surrounding air. Zara's breath caught in her throat. The hairs on the back of her neck stood on end, and she clutched the compass tighter. "We should keep moving."

They pressed on, the sun dipping lower, casting a faint orange glow across the

landscape. The compass needle had finally begun to settle, pointing firmly toward the ground beneath their feet. Grandpa Ben led them to a stone slab, slightly lifted at one corner, as if inviting them to look closer. He knelt beside it, pressing his hand against the cold surface, his movements sure and deliberate, like someone who had done this before.

"I've heard whispers about this place," Grandpa Ben said quietly, almost to himself. "A secret chamber, hidden beneath Stonehenge. My grandfather always spoke of an ancient secret buried here. Something the druids didn't want anyone to find. And now…" His voice trailed off as his hand pushed harder against the stone. "Now I think we're about to find it."

Max and Lottie stood back, their eyes wide with anticipation and fear. Max's mind raced with the possibilities—treasures, ancient artifacts, something dangerous. He could almost feel his heart pounding in his throat. Lottie, on the other hand, felt a knot of anxiety tightening in her stomach. She shifted her weight from one foot to the other, the cool wind cutting through her clothes.

Zara, however, felt her pulse quicken with a different emotion. Excitement. This was what they'd been searching for. They were on the verge of uncovering something ancient, something powerful. The compass's pull was stronger now, almost vibrating in her hand.

With a grunt, Grandpa Ben and Max heaved the stone slab aside, revealing a dark passage that sloped into the earth. The air that rose from below was thick, musty, and still, as though it hadn't been disturbed in centuries. A faint metallic tang lingered in the air.

Lottie took a step back, her face pale. "Are we really going down there?"

"We have to," Zara said, her voice steady, though her heartbeat quickened. "This is why the compass brought us here."

Max nodded, though his hands trembled slightly as he wiped them on his jeans. "We've come this far. We can't turn back now."

Grandpa Ben stood, brushing the dirt from his hands, his face serious, but there

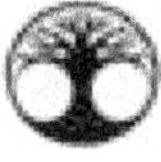

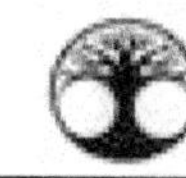

was something else in his eyes—a flicker of worry, maybe fear. He looked at the three of them, his voice gruff but soft. "Once we go down there, there's no telling what we'll find. But know this—whatever's been buried beneath Stonehenge, the druids didn't want it falling into the wrong hands." He paused, his gaze lingering on each of them. "And it's something we must protect."

A chill ran through Zara. The sense of awe that had filled her earlier was now tainted with a creeping sense of danger. She glanced back at the stone circle, half-expecting to see a shadow moving between the stones, watching them. Was someone—or something—following their every step?

She turned back to the passage. No. She couldn't stop now. Not when they were so close.

As they began their descent into the ancient passage, the darkness seemed to swallow them. The air was thick and cold, pressing in from all sides. Zara stole a glance at Grandpa Ben. His face was set in hard lines, but his eyes glimmered with both excitement and caution.

He wasn't just their guide—he was a part of this. Whatever secrets lay beneath Stonehenge, Grandpa Ben was tied to them in ways he hadn't yet revealed.

And as they ventured further into the unknown, Zara felt a certainty deep in her bones: the secrets of Stonehenge were far greater than any of them had imagined.

Chapter 6: The Passage of Trials

The air seemed to grow thicker, denser with every step they took as they ventured deeper into the underground tunnel. The narrow walls pressed in around them, slick with moisture and exuding a damp, musty scent that carried the weight of time. Ancient stone, cold and jagged, scraped against Max's hand as he trailed his fingers along the wall, feeling the rough edges as if they were

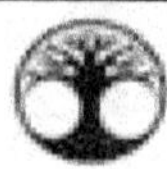

sharpened by centuries. The cold bit into his skin, sending an involuntary shiver through his arm. He glanced over at Lottie, her expression intense as she studied the old map in her hands, her brow furrowed with concentration, each line etched into her face betraying the effort she was putting into making sure they didn't lose their way.

"I don't like this place," Lottie muttered, her voice quiet but steady. There was an edge to her tone, one that only Max would have noticed. They had known each other for too long to miss the subtleties. "It feels… wrong."

Max nodded in agreement, though he didn't say anything. The unease had been gnawing at him since they had first descended into the tunnel. There was something about this place that seemed to breathe with its own malevolent life. It was as though the very walls were watching them, the ancient stone holding secrets too dark to reveal. But as much as the tension wound tighter inside him, his gaze kept being drawn to the glowing compass in his hand. The light from the compass was growing brighter now, pulsing faintly in a rhythm that mirrored the beat of his own heart. A warmth surged through his fingers, spreading up his arm, radiating from the compass as if it were alive, as if it knew something they didn't.

He couldn't help but wonder—what kind of magic powered it? What ancient force had crafted such a thing, and for what purpose? Was it really guiding them to safety, or were they being lured deeper into danger? The thought twisted in his mind like a knot he couldn't unravel. What if the compass wasn't helping them at all? What if it was leading them into a trap, playing them like pawns in a game far older and more dangerous than they could understand?

Max's thoughts churned with doubt, every step forward feeling heavier, more precarious. It was like walking a tightrope, the excitement of adventure pulling him one way, the looming threat of peril pulling him another. His grip on the compass tightened, and the warmth it emitted began to grow uncomfortable, almost burning against his skin. He stole a glance at Lottie, who was walking slightly ahead of him, her eyes still scanning the map. She seemed so sure of herself, so focused. She trusted him. That trust weighed heavily on his shoulders; a responsibility he wasn't sure he was ready to bear. Lottie looked up to him, and

the thought that he could somehow let her down made the tightness in his chest even worse.

"Max," Grandpa Ben's voice, deep and steady, broke through his spiraling thoughts. The old man's eyes were sharp, scanning the narrow passage ahead. There was a calmness about him, an unshakable certainty in the way he carried himself, even here in the depths of the unknown. "Stay alert. This is where the real trials begin."

Max's gaze flickered toward him, curiosity mingling with the ever-present unease. Grandpa Ben always seemed to know more than he let on. There was something in the way he moved, the way his steps never faltered, as though he had walked this path before. How much did the old man really know? How many secrets was he keeping, not just from them, but from himself? Max felt a twinge of regret for not asking more questions earlier, before they were so deep into this. But now, it was too late to turn back.

Lottie, who had been silent for a while, suddenly spoke up, breaking the tense quiet. "What if we go around instead of straight through?" she suggested, her voice calm despite the circumstances. She held up the map, her finger tracing a faint line. "The map shows a side route that might avoid whatever traps are waiting for us."

Max blinked, surprised by her observation. He hadn't noticed the side path on the map. Leaning over her shoulder, he saw the faint lines she was pointing to—delicate, almost invisible, a hidden route that could very well save them. "That could work," he admitted, impressed by her sharp eye. Lottie had always been the quick thinker, and in moments like this, he was grateful for it. "It might be safer."

Grandpa Ben nodded approvingly. "Good thinking, Lottie. It's always wise to consider all options."

With a renewed sense of purpose, Lottie led the way into the narrow side passage, her confidence a reassuring presence even in the dim light of the tunnel. But the air didn't feel any less oppressive. The sense of danger still hung thick around them, heavy and unavoidable. The walls seemed to press in tighter as

they moved through the narrow passage, the stone ceiling feeling lower with every step. Max's heart pounded in his chest, the rhythmic pulsing of the compass matching the beat of his fear. The light from the compass pulsed again, casting eerie, shifting shadows on the slick walls. For a moment, Max thought he saw something move in the darkness—a flicker of shadow too fast to track. His breath caught in his throat.

The stone beneath his feet shifted suddenly, and for a split second, his heart leapt into his throat. He froze, fear coursing through him. Had he triggered something? Was this the moment the trap would spring?

Nothing happened.

The close call sent a chill down his spine, a reminder of how precarious their situation was. He couldn't afford to be careless. None of them could. He glanced at Lottie again, her determined expression unwavering as she continued to guide them through the passage. She was growing—no longer just the little sister following in his footsteps, but someone who was beginning to lead, someone making decisions that could save them all. The realization hit him like a cold shock. She was becoming someone he could trust, someone they all could trust.

The compass pulsed brighter again, its warmth creeping up Max's arm, spreading further than before. It wasn't just a tool anymore. It felt alive, ancient, and connected to something far older than anything they had encountered. Was it truly trying to help them, or was it controlling them, manipulating their choices without them realizing it?

As they approached the platform ahead, the air grew warmer, charged with an invisible energy that seemed to hum through the ground beneath their feet. The very earth seemed to vibrate with anticipation, as if something was waiting for them, something they couldn't see but could definitely feel. Max held the compass higher, feeling its heartbeat sync with his own, the connection between them deepening in a way that both comforted and terrified him.

"Do you feel that?" Max asked, his voice quieter than he intended. There was a tremble in his words that he couldn't quite hide.

Lottie stepped closer, her hand hovering near the compass but not quite touching it. "It's warm... like it's guiding us," she whispered, awe creeping into her voice. "But guiding us where?"

Max didn't have an answer. And that was what worried him the most. He had followed the compass for so long, trusting its light, but now he wasn't even sure why anymore. He wasn't chasing treasure or glory. It was something deeper, something tied to the legacy of his family—a legacy he was only beginning to understand. Was he trying to prove something to himself, or was it more than that? Was the compass tied to something ancient, a past neither he nor Grandpa Ben had fully spoken of yet?

Grandpa Ben's voice broke through his thoughts again, low and steady as always. "Keep moving, Max. The real danger is just ahead."

Max swallowed hard, his mouth dry. His feet felt heavier with every step, as though the very air was trying to hold him back. As they neared the platform, the stone beneath them shifted again, the low grinding sound echoing through the cavern like a warning. The vibration in the air intensified, and for a moment, Max felt dizzy, the world tilting slightly as his heart raced.

Chapter 7: The Guardians of the Henge

The narrow passageway seemed to stretch on forever, twisting and turning through the earth. The deeper Max, Lottie, and Grandpa Ben ventured, the more the air seemed to hum with an ancient energy. The glow of the compass provided the only light, casting eerie shadows on the rough stone walls.

Max's thoughts were spinning. What if this was a mistake? The compass had led them so far, but every step deeper into the earth brought a new wave of doubt. What if it led them into danger they weren't ready for? He glanced at Lottie, who usually charged ahead without hesitation, but tonight, even she seemed quiet, sticking close to his side.

 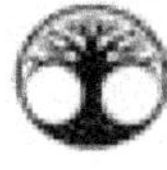 

His throat tightened. If Lottie was nervous, that was a bad sign.

"Are you okay?" Max whispered, glancing at her. His voice felt small in the heavy silence.

Lottie shrugged, her hand gripping his sleeve a little tighter. "I guess. But doesn't this place feel… off to you?"

Max nodded. He couldn't shake the feeling that something was watching them, waiting. "Yeah. But we'll figure it out. We always do."

Suddenly, the passage widened, opening into a large, dimly lit chamber. The air here was thick and still, as if it hadn't been disturbed for centuries. Max felt the hairs on the back of his neck stand on end. Something—no, someone—was watching them.

"Stay close," Grandpa Ben whispered, his voice barely audible. His hand tightened around his walking stick, which Max now realized wasn't just for show; it was a sturdy piece of wood, carved with strange symbols that Max had never noticed before. How had he missed that?

Lottie pressed against Max's side. "What do you think is in here?" she whispered; her voice shaky. It felt more like she was thinking aloud than really asking.

Max swallowed; his mouth dry. "I don't know." For once, the adventure didn't feel exciting. It felt… dangerous.

Before he could say more, the light from the compass flickered, and the shadows around them shifted. From the darkness, figures began to emerge, moving slowly into the dim light. Max's breath caught in his throat as he realized these weren't just any figures—they were the Guardians of the Henge.

The Guardians were unlike anything Max had ever seen. They were tall and imposing, their bodies a strange mix of human and animal features. One had the head of an owl with large, golden eyes that glowed in the dark. Another had the body of a man but with the hind legs of a stag, hooves clacking against the stone floor. A third was shrouded in a cloak of feathers, its face hidden, but with talons

for hands that gleamed in the faint light.

These creatures weren't just protectors; they were the living embodiment of the ancient magic woven into Stonehenge thousands of years ago.

"Who dares to trespass on the sacred ground of the Henge?" the owl-headed Guardian spoke, its voice deep and resonant, echoing off the walls of the chamber. "Speak or face the consequences."

Max swallowed hard, his heart pounding in his chest. He looked at Grandpa Ben, who gave him a slight nod, urging him to speak.

Max took a deep breath. "We… we're just trying to understand Stonehenge. The compass led us here. We didn't come to cause trouble."

The Guardians exchanged glances, their eyes narrowing as they studied the trio. The stag-legged Guardian stepped forward, lowering its head slightly, as if sniffing the air.

"The compass," it said, its voice a strange mix of human speech and animal growl. "The Druid's Compass. It has not been seen in this place for many generations. Why have you brought it here?"

Max hesitated, but Lottie, surprising him, stepped forward. "It's been pulling us here the whole time. We didn't have a choice." Her voice cracked slightly, but her defiance was clear.

The feathered Guardian tilted its head, its talons clicking together. "The Compass chooses its bearers wisely. But the path you seek is not one of ease or safety. There are trials you must face, tests to prove your worth. Only then can you uncover the secrets that lie within the heart of the Henge."

Max's stomach twisted. Tests? Trials? He hadn't expected this. They'd come so far, but now the reality of the situation hit him. He wasn't ready for this. But the look in the Guardians' eyes told him there was no turning back.

"What kind of trials?" Max asked, his voice betraying a hint of fear.

The owl-headed Guardian raised its wings, and the chamber filled with a soft, golden light. "Three trials you must pass. The Trial of Knowledge, the Trial of Courage, and the Trial of Heart. Each one will test you in a different way. Only if you succeed in all three will you be deemed worthy to continue your journey."

Grandpa Ben stepped forward, his face serious, eyes scanning the Guardians with a look Max hadn't seen before. "We are ready. Tell us what we must do."

Max shot his grandfather a glance. Are we? But Grandpa Ben's expression remained resolute, his grip tight on the carved staff. A sinking feeling crept into Max's gut—how much more did Grandpa Ben know about this than he was letting on?

The Guardians exchanged another glance, then the stag-legged Guardian spoke. "The first trial, the Trial of Knowledge, will test your understanding of the ancient ways. You must answer a riddle, one that has confounded even the wisest of sages. Fail, and you will be turned back. Succeed, and you will move on to the next trial."

The owl-headed Guardian's eyes glowed brighter, casting golden light across the chamber. Its voice boomed, echoing off the walls, "Listen carefully:

I speak without a mouth and hear without ears. I have no body, but I come alive with the wind. What am I?"

Max's mind spun as he repeated the riddle to himself, trying to make sense of the cryptic words. He stole a glance at Lottie. Her face was scrunched in concentration, and her lips moved silently as if she were mouthing the words over and over again. She tapped her chin, deep in thought, but the puzzle seemed to elude her as well.

"What do you think it means?" Max whispered, his voice barely audible in the vast, eerie chamber. The pressure of the Guardians' expectant gaze made it hard to think straight. They couldn't afford to get this wrong.

Lottie tilted her head, her brow furrowing. "It's something... something that moves with the wind, but it doesn't have a body. Like... maybe a spirit? But it

doesn't really speak or hear..."

Max frowned. That didn't seem right, but he wasn't sure what did. The riddle was gnawing at the edges of his mind, but the answer danced just out of reach. "It has to be something simple," he murmured, half to himself. "Something we've seen or heard before..."

Lottie nodded slowly. "It hears without ears... and it speaks without a mouth. But how is that possible?"

Max's mind flashed back to the wind that had whispered through the stones earlier, the way it seemed to carry voices on it. Maybe that was it... No, it couldn't be just the wind itself. There was something more.

"I think it's..." Lottie started but then trailed off. "Wait, it's not just the wind. What if it's the sound that the wind carries?"

Max felt a spark of recognition flicker. "Like... an echo!" he blurted out, louder than he intended.

Lottie's eyes lit up. "Yes, that's it! An echo! It doesn't have a mouth, but it speaks. And it doesn't hear, but it repeats whatever it hears."

Max felt a wave of relief wash over him as the pieces clicked together. "It's an echo," he said, this time more confidently. He turned to Grandpa Ben, who had been watching them with a knowing smile.

Grandpa Ben gave a slow nod. "Yes," he said, his voice calm and steady. "The answer is an echo."

For a moment, the Guardians were silent, their eyes glowing brighter as they exchanged glances. Then, the owl-headed Guardian dipped its head. "You have answered correctly. The Trial of Knowledge is passed."

Max let out a breath he hadn't realized he'd been holding. One trial down, two to go.

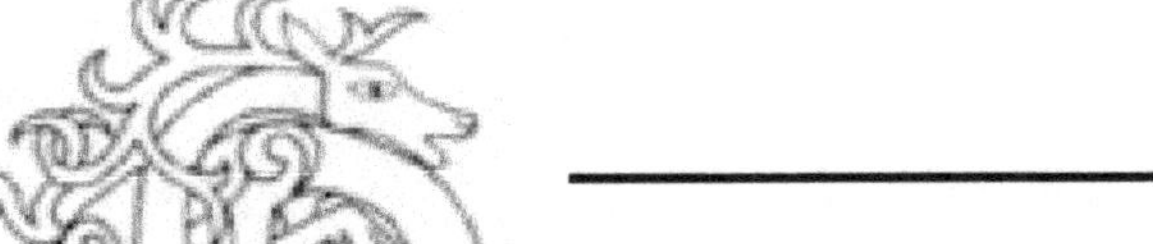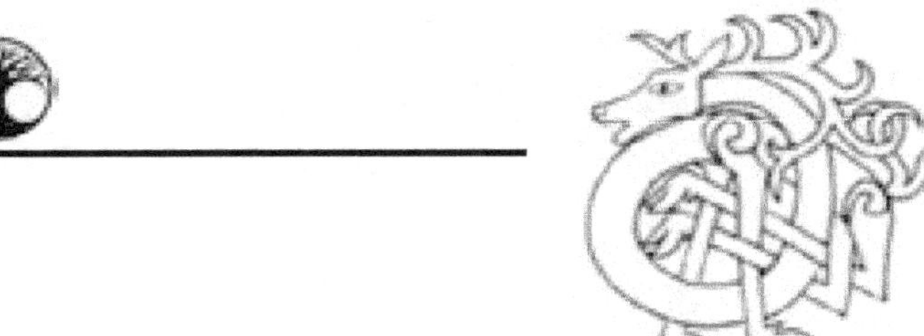

The second trial, the feathered Guardian said, "is the Trial of Courage. You must face your deepest fear. Each of you will be tested, and only if you conquer your fear will you be allowed to continue."

Max felt a chill run down his spine. Face his deepest fear? He wasn't ready for that. He didn't even know what his deepest fear was. Or... did he?

Beside him, Lottie's eyes widened. She stepped closer to Max, her hand brushing against his. "Deepest fear?" she whispered, her voice trembling. "I'm not... I mean, I didn't sign up for this!"

Max swallowed hard. Lottie was always the brave one, the first to jump into anything without hesitation. If she was afraid, then what chance did he have?

"We'll figure it out," Max said, trying to sound more confident than he felt. "We always do."

Lottie looked up at him, her eyes searching his face for reassurance. "Do you think we'll have to do this... alone?"

Max opened his mouth to answer, but before he could speak, the chamber around them began to shift and change. The walls seemed to melt away, and suddenly, Max found himself alone in a dark, endless void. The air was thick and oppressive, and a cold sweat broke out on his forehead.

He spun around, his heart hammering in his chest. "Lottie? Grandpa Ben?" His voice echoed into the emptiness, swallowed by the void. "Lottie!".

No answer. Only the suffocating darkness that surrounded him. Max's breath came in short gasps as panic clawed at his throat. This isn't real. It's just part of the trial. Stay calm, Max. Stay calm.

From the darkness, a figure emerged—a shadowy form that looked just like him. But its eyes were hollow, and its face twisted into a cruel smile. Max's heart sank. He knew what this was. It wasn't just his shadow. It was every doubt he'd ever had, every fear he'd ever tried to bury.

"You're not strong enough," the shadow whispered, its voice an eerie reflection of

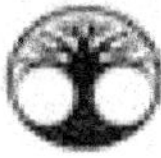

his own. "You'll fail. You're not brave; you're just pretending to be. You're scared. You've always been scared."

Max clenched his fists, his knuckles white. The words burrowed into him like sharp thorns. Is that true? Images flashed before him—times he'd let Lottie take the lead because he didn't want to mess up. That one moment when he'd frozen in fear during their last adventure, leaving her in danger. He had always told himself he was just being careful. But what if... what if he really had been scared all along?

The shadow hissed again, stepping closer, its voice growing louder. "You've failed before. You'll fail again. Remember when...?"

Images flooded his mind—times he'd stumbled, failed, disappointed those around him. A tidal wave of shame hit him, threatening to drown him. I've always been scared. Is that all I am?

No. Max shook his head, trying to push the thoughts away. No. That's not true. I'm not just my failures. They don't define me. He thought of Lottie, of Grandpa Ben. They believed in him. And he believed in himself, too.

"You're wrong," Max said, his voice growing stronger, though his heart still pounded. "I'm not afraid of you. I'm not just my failures. I am strong. And I will succeed."

The shadow sneered, its twisted smile fading as it lunged at him, trying to pull him into the darkness. But Max stood his ground. He wouldn't let it consume him. The moment the shadow touched him, it dissolved into mist, and the darkness began to lift.

Slowly, the void faded away, and Max found himself back in the chamber, his chest heaving as though he'd just run a mile. The Guardians were still there, watching him with eyes that gleamed in approval.

Max looked around, relief flooding him as he saw Lottie reappearing too. Her face

was pale, and she was trembling slightly, but when their eyes met, she gave him a small, shaky smile.

"You okay?" Max asked softly, stepping closer to her.

Lottie nodded, though her voice wavered when she spoke. "Yeah. I... I don't really want to talk about it, but... yeah."

Max gave her hand a reassuring squeeze. "You did great, Lottie. We're almost there."

"The Trial of Courage is passed," the stag-legged Guardian said, its voice filled with approval. "You have proven your bravery."

The final trial, the owl-headed Guardian said, "is the Trial of Heart. This will test your compassion, your kindness, and your willingness to sacrifice for others. You must choose between saving yourself and saving those you care about."

As the Guardian spoke, a door opened in the wall of the chamber, revealing a long, dark tunnel. At the end of the tunnel, Max could see a faint light and hear the distant sound of someone crying out for help. The sound echoed through the passage, tugging at his heart.

"Only one of you may enter," the owl-headed Guardian continued. "Choose wisely."

Max's heart pounded as he looked at Lottie and Grandpa Ben. He didn't want to leave them, but he knew what he had to do. His legs felt like lead, and every part of him screamed to stay by their side, but the faint cries of the person trapped in the tunnel gnawed at him. Could he really walk away from someone in need?

Lottie looked at him, her expression torn. "Max... are you sure? Maybe we should—"

Max shook his head, cutting her off. "No, Lottie. It has to be me." He tried to steady his voice, but his heart raced. "You've always been the brave one, leading

us through most of this journey. But this time… this one's mine." He gave her a small, reassuring smile, even though his insides twisted with uncertainty.

Lottie frowned. "But… what if something happens? What if you can't make it back?"

Max clenched his fists, forcing himself to stay calm. "I don't know. But if I don't try, I'll never forgive myself." He met her gaze. "I have to go. I need to do this."

Grandpa Ben stepped forward, resting a hand on Max's shoulder. "This journey was always yours, Max. You've shown great strength already. Trust in yourself."

Max gave his grandfather a grateful nod. The weight of his words settled on Max's shoulders like a mantle he wasn't sure he could carry, but he had to try. There was no turning back now.

Without waiting for a response, Max stepped into the tunnel. The air was cold and damp, and the sound of crying grew louder as he moved forward. His heart ached with each step. What if this was a trap? What if he was walking into something he couldn't handle?

The passage felt like it was closing in on him, the dim light at the end barely flickering. Was it getting darker, or was that just his fear trying to swallow him whole?

You can't stop now. Max took a deep breath, forcing himself to move forward. His thoughts raced, the weight of the trial pressing down on him. What if I can't save them? What if I fail and leave Lottie and Grandpa behind?

Finally, he reached the end of the tunnel and found a small, dimly lit chamber. In the centre of the room was a young boy, no older than Lottie, trapped under a pile of heavy stones. The boy's face was pale, his cheeks streaked with dirt and tears, and his eyes were wide with terror.

"Help me," the boy pleaded, his voice weak, reaching out towards Max. "Please, help me."

Max's heart twisted in his chest. The boy's voice reminded him of Lottie, of the

time she had been in danger, and he had hesitated. But there was no hesitation now. There couldn't be.

Max dropped to his knees beside the boy, his hands trembling as he touched the heavy stones. "I'm going to get you out of here," Max said, though his voice shook with doubt. The stones looked impossible to move, far heavier than anything he'd ever lifted before.

The boy's small hand clung to Max's sleeve. "It hurts," he whimpered, his eyes filled with fear. "Please don't leave me."

Max's throat tightened. He gritted his teeth and began to lift the first stone. His muscles strained with the effort, every fiber in his body protesting, but he couldn't stop. This boy needed him. He couldn't leave him behind.

But as he worked, a voice echoed in his mind, the voice of doubt that had followed him throughout the trials. What if this isn't real? What if this is just part of the trial? What if helping him means failing the test?

Max hesitated for a split second, his hands hovering over the next stone. What if saving the boy isn't the right choice?

But then he heard the boy's soft cry again, saw the fear in his eyes, and every doubt melted away. Real or not, it didn't matter. He couldn't walk away.

"I'll help you," Max said firmly, gripping the next stone and pulling with all his might. His muscles burned, and his arms shook, but slowly, the stones began to shift. The boy cried out in pain, and Max's heart pounded even harder.

You can do this. Keep going. Don't give up.

The stones felt impossibly heavy, and for a moment, doubt gnawed at him again. What if I can't do this? What if I fail here, now, when it matters most?

But Max kept going, refusing to let the doubt take root. He couldn't let this boy suffer. He wouldn't. With one final effort, Max lifted the last stone, freeing the boy.

The boy looked up at Max with tears in his eyes and whispered, "Thank you."

As the boy spoke, the chamber began to fade, and Max found himself back in the main room with Lottie and Grandpa Ben. The Guardians were standing before him, their eyes filled with approval.

"You have passed the Trial of Heart," the owl-headed Guardian said. "You have proven your compassion and your willingness to sacrifice for others. You are worthy."

Max stood there, breathing hard, feeling the weight of what had just happened sink in. He had done it. They had done it. The sense of relief was overwhelming, but something deeper stirred in his chest—something that told him this was only the beginning.

Lottie rushed forward, throwing her arms around him. "Max, I knew you could do it!" she whispered, her voice tight with emotion.

Max hugged her back, his chest tight with emotion. "I couldn't have done it without you."

Grandpa Ben nodded solemnly, pride gleaming in his eyes. "You've proven yourself, Max. You are ready for what comes next."

Max wasn't so sure about that. The Trials had been hard enough, but something told him the real challenge was still ahead.

"The path ahead is now open to you," the stag-legged Guardian said, gesturing to a door that had appeared in the wall behind them. "Beyond this door lies the final secret of Stonehenge. But remember, the true test lies not in the trials you've faced, but in how you use the knowledge you gain."

Max, Lottie, and Grandpa Ben exchanged determined glances. They had come this far, but Max couldn't shake a feeling deep in his chest. What if the secret wasn't just about Stonehenge? What if it was something more?

He glanced down at the compass, glowing brightly in his hand. It had brought them here for a reason. But was it guiding them to knowledge... or something

they weren't ready for?

Together, they stepped towards the door, the compass still glowing, leading them into the unknown, where the greatest secret of Stonehenge awaited.

Chapter 8: The Starry Night Revelation

The heavy stone door creaked open as Max, Lottie, and Grandpa Ben stepped into the next chamber. The moment they crossed the threshold, the atmosphere seemed to change entirely. A wave of cool air swept past them, carrying with it the scent of damp earth and ancient stone—an almost palpable reminder of how deep beneath the surface they truly were. The faint light from the compass flickered, casting long, eerie shadows across the rough stone walls as they cautiously moved forward. Every sound felt amplified in the silence—each step, each breath, each movement seemed to echo, not just through the chamber, but through the centuries.

This was not just any room. The chamber they had entered was unlike anything they had ever seen before. Above them, a vast dome-shaped ceiling stretched high, its surface speckled with hundreds—no, thousands—of glowing points of light. They weren't just dots; they were stars. As they ventured deeper into the chamber, the stars began to move, swirling and twisting until they formed recognizable constellations—Orion, the Big Dipper, the North Star. It was as though they had left the Earth entirely and stepped into the night sky itself, suspended between worlds.

"This is... unbelievable," Grandpa Ben whispered, his voice reverberating softly off the walls. Awe thickened each word, making them sound almost reverent. "The druids must have used this very chamber to study the stars, to unravel the mysteries of the heavens. We're standing in the heart of their wisdom, the core of their ancient knowledge."

Max felt his chest tighten. His breath caught in his throat as he struggled to pro-

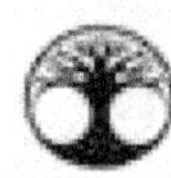

cess the enormity of the moment. The flickering light from the compass seemed to beat in time with his heart, steady but insistent. The vastness of the chamber and the sheer weight of history pressed down on him like an invisible force, almost suffocating. He gripped the compass tighter, the warmth of it radiating through his hand, grounding him amidst the overwhelming sensation. Why me? he thought again, an old question resurfacing with a new intensity. Why this place? Why now?

Beside him, Lottie's wide eyes scanned the stars above. Her face reflected her sense of wonder, but Max knew her too well. Behind the awe was a flicker of apprehension. He could sense her nervous energy, subtle but growing. She shifted on her feet, her lips parting slightly before she spoke, her voice soft but tinged with unease. "But… why here?" she asked, her gaze shifting toward Max and Grandpa Ben. "What does this have to do with Stonehenge? I mean, why would the druids build all of this here?"

Her question hung in the air, echoing Max's own racing thoughts. Before he could answer, the compass in his hand flared with a sudden, blinding light. The needle spun wildly, its tip coming to rest, unwavering, on a point in the centre of the chamber. Max's pulse quickened. There was no doubt—they were being guided by something far older and far wiser than any of them could comprehend.

At the room's heart stood a tall, intricately carved stone pillar. Every inch of its surface was adorned with ancient runes and symbols, their meanings lost to time, but their importance undeniable. A smooth, round crystal sat at the pillar's peak, glowing faintly, resonating with the same light as the stars above. As Max drew closer, he felt the compass pulse in his hand, a rhythmic beat urging him forward.

"This…" Grandpa Ben began, his voice trembling with reverence, "this is the true heart of Stonehenge." He stepped toward the pillar, his fingers barely brushing its edge. His usually steady hands shook ever so slightly. "The druids constructed Stonehenge around this. They harnessed the power of the stars and the earth to create something beyond our understanding. Something… extraordinary."

Max stepped toward the pillar, the warmth from the compass intensifying with

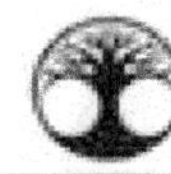

every step. The crystal atop the pillar glowed brighter, and once again, the stars above shifted, this time forming a swirling pattern Max couldn't recognize.

"Look!" Lottie's voice broke the silence, trembling with a mixture of fear and excitement. She pointed upward. "The stars… they're changing again!"

Max and Grandpa Ben followed her gaze. The stars had rearranged themselves into a spiral, and at the centre of the spiral, one single star shone brighter than all the rest. Its light cast a beam directly onto the crystal. A deep hum filled the chamber, a sound that wasn't just heard but felt, reverberating through Max's very bones. Beneath his feet, the ground seemed alive, pulsing with a rhythmic energy that matched the flickering compass in his hand.

"This…" Grandpa Ben's voice was barely a whisper, "this is the Starry Night Revelation. The druids believed that when the stars aligned in this pattern, the true purpose of Stonehenge would be revealed. But no one has witnessed it—until now."

Max felt the weight of the moment press down on him, heavier than anything he had ever experienced. The compass pulsed in his hand, almost too hot to hold now. His mind raced, spinning with doubts. Why me? Why now? The thought repeated itself, louder each time. What if I fail? What if I'm not supposed to do this? He was just Max—no one special, no great hero. But here he stood on the brink of something unimaginable.

The light from the crystal grew blinding, and the runes on the pillar began to glow, one by one, their ancient energy lighting up the room. This is too much, Max thought, overwhelmed by the responsibility. I didn't ask for this. He hesitated, feeling the knot of uncertainty tighten in his stomach. His mind reeled with questions, doubts, fears. But there was no turning back now.

Max swallowed hard and stepped forward, ignoring the rising tide of doubt. He knelt at the base of the pillar, placing the compass carefully against the ancient stone. The moment it made contact, the crystal erupted with light, flooding the chamber with a brilliance that momentarily blinded him. The runes cascaded to life, each one lighting up in rapid succession, sending a surge of energy through

 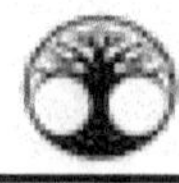 

the very air.

As the light intensified, the stars above began to move faster, swirling in chaotic beauty. From the light, images began to emerge—ancient druids standing beneath the night sky, their arms raised as if in communion with the stars themselves. The stones of Stonehenge glowed with an inner fire, pulsating like the heart of the Earth.

But it wasn't just Stonehenge. The images shifted, showing a druid holding a compass much like the one in Max's hand. The figure was tall, imposing, but with eyes that radiated kindness and wisdom. His gaze seemed to pierce through time itself, settling on Max. It was as though the druid recognized him, acknowledged him.

Max's heart pounded in his chest. I didn't choose this, he thought. But it's chosen me.

Before Max could dwell on his doubts, the stars on the ceiling spun faster and faster, rearranging into a map. Each glowing star connected with lines of light, forming an intricate web that stretched across the entire world. "Look!" Lottie whispered. "Those points—they're ancient sites!"

Max's heart raced as he recognized them—Machu Picchu, the pyramids of Giza, the Great Wall of China. Each site connected by lines of shimmering light. They weren't just random points—they were part of something bigger, something global.

Grandpa Ben stepped forward; his eyes wide with realization. "Stonehenge isn't just a monument," he said, his voice grave. "It's a nexus. A hub that channels the power of these sacred places."

Max shivered, the magnitude of their discovery dawning on him. "It's like… a circuit," he whispered. "Connecting all these places, balancing the Earth's energy."

The images of ancient civilizations—druids, Egyptians, Incas—faded into the stars, leaving behind a sense of both wonder and impending danger. Max felt the weight of it all. This wasn't just a discovery—it was a warning. If someone else

knew about this...

"The compass..." Lottie's voice was almost a whisper. "It's the key to unlocking these places, isn't it?"

Grandpa Ben's face darkened. "That's why it chose you, Max. To protect this knowledge. If it falls into the wrong hands..."

Max's mind raced with images of what could happen if this power were misused. This knowledge could destroy everything. The compass had chosen him—but at what cost?

As the light dimmed and the stars returned to their calm glow, Max knew one thing: their journey was far from over. Somewhere, in the shadows, forces may already be moving to claim the power they had just uncovered.

Chapter 9: The Druid's Legacy

The cool air of the chamber clung to them as Max, Lottie, and Grandpa Ben retraced their steps back through the winding passages of Stonehenge. The revelation they had just witnessed hung in the air like an unspoken promise—a connection to something ancient and powerful, a legacy that had now been passed down to them. But it also weighed on Max's mind like an invisible burden, one he wasn't sure he was ready for.

As they emerged from the dark tunnels into the soft light of dawn, the stone circle of Stonehenge greeted them with a quiet, reverent stillness. The sky above was tinged with the first hues of morning, the stars fading into the soft blue as the sun prepared to rise. But in Max's mind, the image of the starry chamber and the glowing runes was still vivid, as if it had imprinted itself onto his very soul. He glanced at Lottie beside him; her face was thoughtful, but he could see a glimmer of awe in her eyes as she absorbed the enormity of what they had uncovered.

Max knelt before the ancient carvings, tracing his fingers over the worn grooves. This was what he had been searching for all along—a purpose. Memories of endless days back in the village, feeling lost and directionless, bubbled up in his mind. He'd spent years looking for answers that never came. But now, with the druids' knowledge at his fingertips, he understood. All those years of doubt had led him here, to this moment. For the first time in his life, he felt like he belonged.

But that belonging came with responsibility, and the weight of it was beginning to settle on his shoulders.

Grandpa Ben leaned on his walking stick, gazing thoughtfully at the ancient stones that surrounded them. He looked tired; Max noticed—older than he had before—but there was a fire in his eyes that hadn't dimmed. "We've uncovered something extraordinary," he said quietly. "But there's one more piece to this puzzle—something the druids left behind, something they wanted us to find."

Max looked at the compass in his hand. The needle was still, pointing north as it always did, but the warmth he felt from it was more than just physical. It was as if the compass itself was alive, aware of its purpose and their journey. It throbbed gently in his palm, almost in time with his heartbeat.

"What do you mean, Grandpa?" Lottie asked, her voice soft in the stillness of the early morning. Max could hear a note of apprehension there, as though she wasn't sure she wanted to hear the answer.

Grandpa Ben turned to them, his eyes filled with a mix of pride and anticipation, but also something deeper—something like worry. "The druids knew that their knowledge and power would eventually fade into legend. But they also knew that one day, someone worthy would come along to inherit their legacy. That's why they created the compass—not just to guide us to the secrets of Stonehenge, but to something even greater."

He gestured towards a small outcrop of stones on the far side of the circle, partially hidden by the shadows of the massive Saracens. "There's a place—a final chamber—that holds the last piece of the druids' legacy. The compass will guide

us there."

Max felt a thrill of anticipation, but it was tempered with a strange unease. He exchanged a glance with Lottie, whose brow furrowed. She seemed hesitant, as though she wasn't sure if they should keep pushing forward. He knew what she was thinking—what if they weren't meant to disturb whatever had been left behind?

"The journey isn't over yet," Grandpa Ben continued. "There's still more to discover, more to understand. But we must tread carefully. The knowledge we've found so far is only the beginning."

Max nodded, gripping the compass tighter, though the unease he felt continued to grow. There was still more to uncover, but now the weight of that responsibility pressed heavier on him. It was no longer just about finding something for hImself. He and Lottie were the keepers of something ancient and sacred, and that meant they weren't the only ones who would want it.

With Grandpa Ben leading the way, they made their way across the stone circle. The early morning light cast long shadows across the ground, and the air was filled with the crisp freshness of a new day. As they approached the outcrop, Max noticed that the compass needle had begun to glow faintly, pointing directly at a narrow gap between the stones.

"This is it," Grandpa Ben said, his voice filled with quiet reverence. "The final resting place of the druids' legacy."

Max squeezed through the narrow opening, with Lottie and Grandpa Ben close behind. The passage was tight, but after a few moments, it opened up into a small, circular chamber. Unlike the other chambers they had encountered, this one was simple and unadorned, with smooth stone walls and a single, unadorned altar in the centre.

On the altar sat a small, ancient box, made of dark wood and bound with iron bands. The box was unassuming, but Max could feel the power emanating from it—a quiet, steady pulse that resonated with the warmth of the compass.

The final chamber was deceptively simple. The stone walls were bare, but the air thrummed with a quiet hum, as if the magic here had a pulse of its own. Max noticed the stones beneath his feet were warmer than they should be, like the ground itself had been soaking up centuries of power. The light inside the chamber flickered unnaturally, not like a flame, but more like the soft glow of starlight, casting shifting shadows that seemed to dance to an ancient rhythm.

"This is what they left for us," Grandpa Ben said, stepping forward and gently lifting the box from the altar. He paused for a moment, looking down at the box as though considering the weight of it—not just in his hands, but in his heart. "The druids knew that one day, someone would come who would need their wisdom. This box contains the last of their teachings—their legacy, preserved for those who would follow in their footsteps."

Max and Lottie gathered around as Grandpa Ben carefully opened the box. Inside, nestled in a bed of soft, ancient cloth, was a collection of scrolls, each one meticulously preserved despite the passage of thousands of years. The scrolls were covered in strange symbols and writing that Max didn't recognize, but he could sense their importance, their weight.

"These scrolls," Grandpa Ben murmured, his eyes shining with awe, "contain the druids' final teachings—their knowledge of the stars, the earth, and the ancient magic that binds them together. They are a guide, not just to the secrets of Stonehenge, but to the wisdom that the druids believed was essential for the survival of humanity."

Lottie peered over Grandpa Ben's shoulder; her eyes wide. "What do they say?"

Grandpa Ben gently unrolled one of the scrolls, revealing lines of delicate script interspersed with intricate diagrams of constellations, plants, and ancient symbols. As he began to read aloud, Max felt a sense of wonder and humility wash over him. The symbols on the scroll began to glow, faint at first but growing brighter as Lottie's fingers brushed over them, her curiosity awakening something within the scrolls themselves.

"The druids believed that the world was a living, breathing entity," Grandpa Ben

explained. "They understood that everything in the universe is connected—every star, every tree, every person. They used their knowledge to heal the earth, to guide their people, and to protect the balance of nature."

He looked up at Max and Lottie, his expression serious but weary. "But they also knew that this knowledge could be dangerous if it fell into the wrong hands. That's why they hid it away, waiting for the right time, the right people, to reveal it to."

Max felt a shiver run down his spine. It wasn't just the weight of the knowledge they'd uncovered—it was the feeling that someone, somewhere, was watching. He glanced toward the narrow entrance, his heart suddenly pounding in his chest. Was it paranoia? Or was someone truly following their steps?

Grandpa Ben's eyes flicked toward the entrance too, just for a moment, but it was enough for Max to know he felt it too. They weren't the only ones seeking the druids' wisdom. And not everyone would want it for noble purposes.

Max felt the weight of responsibility settle more heavily on his shoulders. The druids had trusted them with their legacy, their most precious secrets. It was up to them to protect that knowledge, to use it wisely, and to ensure that it was passed down to future generations.

"The compass brought us here," Max said quietly, his voice steady but tinged with uncertainty. "It chose us to carry on the druids' legacy. But how do we do that? How do we protect something so important?"

Grandpa Ben smiled gently, though there was a glint of caution in his eyes. "By living according to the principles that the druids held dear. By respecting the earth, by understanding the stars, and by using this knowledge to help others, not harm them. The compass has guided us this far, and it will continue to guide us as long as we stay true to those values."

Lottie reached out and touched one of the scrolls, her fingers brushing the delicate parchment. "We'll keep the knowledge safe, won't we, Max? We'll make sure it's used for good."

Max nodded, feeling a deep sense of purpose—but also a creeping sense of doubt. "We will, Lottie. We'll protect it, just like the druids did. And when the time is right, we'll pass it on to those who come after us."

Together, they carefully returned the scrolls to the box and closed the lid. The chamber around them seemed to hum with approval, as if the spirits of the druids themselves were watching over them, guiding them on their journey.

As they made their way back out of the chamber and into the light of the new day, Max felt a sense of peace and fulfillment. They had completed their quest, uncovered the secrets of Stonehenge, and inherited the legacy of the ancient druids. But more than that, they had discovered their own strength, courage, and wisdom.

Yet, as the sun rose higher in the sky, Max couldn't help but feel the weight of what they had uncovered. He understood the power of the druids' knowledge, but he also realized how fragile it was in the hands of the world. What if people refuse to believe? The world was full of different beliefs, ancient teachings passed down from different faiths. The druids' legacy had the power to change everything, to challenge the foundations of what so many believed. Would people be willing to accept this new truth, or would they reject it out of fear, clinging to the old ways?

Max shivered at the thought. There would be those who wouldn't want this message to get out—those who feared the power of this knowledge because it threatened everything they knew. The druids had warned them that their teachings could disrupt the very beliefs that structured society. If the truth were exposed, it might make some of the sacred texts and beliefs in the world seem less important, even irrelevant. And that was a message that wouldn't sit well with many.

The man who had delivered the compass to Max, so mysteriously, flashed through his mind. Who was he? Why did he give me the compass? That feeling of being watched returned, a shadow hanging over him, prickling at the back of his neck. Was someone out there, waiting for them to slip up, to reveal the druids' secrets?

 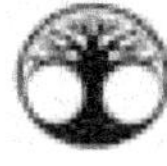 

Max knew they weren't alone. He, Lottie, and Grandpa Ben had taken the first steps toward something monumental, but they would have to be careful. This knowledge could change everything—or it could destroy them.

As they walked away from Stonehenge, the compass tucked safely in Max's pocket and the box of scrolls in Grandpa Ben's hands, Max looked up at the sky. The stars had faded, but he knew they were still there, watching over them, guiding them, just as they always had.

The druids' legacy was now theirs to protect, and with the compass as their guide, Max, Lottie, and Grandpa Ben knew that they were ready to face whatever challenges the future might hold. But the question of who else might be watching remained unanswered, casting a long shadow over their newfound purpose.

And as they walked on, Max couldn't help but smile—albeit cautiously. The adventure might have ended, but the journey was far from over.

Chapter 10: The Choice

The sun hovered just above the horizon, casting long, golden rays across the towering stones of Stonehenge. Each beam painted the ancient monument with a warm glow, yet the air remained crisp, biting at their skin with the chill of early morning. The dampness of dew-soaked grass clung to their boots, and the scent of wet earth filled their lungs. It felt as though the entire landscape held its breath, waiting—expecting—some monumental shift. The stillness wasn't just of the air, but of time itself, a sense of pause as if the earth was holding back to witness what came next.

Max, Lottie, and Grandpa Ben emerged from the hidden chamber; their expressions weighed down by the decision that lay ahead. Each of them carried the weight of discovery, the knowledge they had unearthed pulling at their minds and

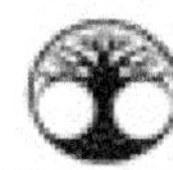

hearts. The beauty of the scene around them seemed distant, overshadowed by the gravity of the choice that loomed over them like a storm cloud. The ancient stones, once so awe-inspiring, now seemed like silent sentinels, watching them, judging them.

Max's fingers instinctively brushed the compass in his pocket, feeling its warmth seep through the fabric—a steady pulse of power and responsibility that only he seemed to feel. It had grown warmer since they had uncovered the scrolls, as if it too had absorbed the secrets of the druids. Each beat of its pulse resonated within him, a constant reminder that this decision rested squarely on his shoulders. They gathered around one of the larger stones, the ancient scrolls resting in a weathered box at their feet. The silence that settled over them wasn't empty. It hummed with the magnitude of all they had uncovered, all they had yet to understand.

Lottie glanced between Max and Grandpa Ben; her eyes wide with apprehension. "What happens now?" she asked softly, breaking the stillness. Her voice barely rose above a whisper, yet the question seemed to echo off the stones around them. "We've found all this knowledge, but what are we supposed to do with it?" There was a note of desperation in her voice, a plea for certainty, for direction. The enormity of their discovery weighed on her too, but Max could tell she was looking to him for guidance, for leadership, and that only intensified the pressure building within him.

Grandpa Ben knelt beside the box, his hands trembling slightly as he lifted the lid to reveal the scrolls once more. The sight of them stirred something deep within Max, a mixture of awe and dread. The weight of the druids' legacy was almost too much to bear. These scrolls held answers—perhaps even solutions to problems the world hadn't yet realized it faced. But they also held something else: danger. And now, a new layer of mystery surrounded the compass in his pocket. What more did it know? What had it led them to uncover that they hadn't yet grasped?

"There are a few paths we could take," Grandpa Ben began, his voice calm but with an edge of uncertainty that Max had never heard before. He cleared his

throat, as if bracing himself for what he was about to say. "We could keep this knowledge hidden, guard it like the druids did, making sure it never falls into the wrong hands. They hid it away for a reason—they understood how dangerous it could be if misused." His eyes darted to Max, as though silently conveying the weight of that danger.

Max's gaze fell on the scrolls, and a tightness settled in his chest. To hide them away would be the safest option, yes. The knowledge they contained was powerful, far beyond what the modern world could comprehend. But the thought of locking it away, of denying the world the wisdom it could offer, felt like a betrayal of everything they had fought for. And yet, could he trust the world to use this knowledge wisely? His mind swirled with questions, doubts, and the nagging fear that no matter what choice they made, it might not be the right one.

"Or" Grandpa Ben continued, his voice growing more thoughtful, more hesitant, "we could share the knowledge. Help people reconnect with the earth, the stars, and the ancient magic that binds them. But…" He paused, glancing up at Max, his brow deeply furrowed. "If we do that, we risk it being twisted, exploited for reasons the druids never intended. If the wrong people got hold of this, the consequences could be catastrophic."

Lottie shifted uncomfortably, her arms crossed tightly, her frown deepening. She opened her mouth to speak, then closed it again, as if unsure of how to voice the questions running through her mind. Finally, her voice broke through the tension, strong but laced with uncertainty. "But if we don't share it, won't the world just keep forgetting?" Her words hung in the air; their weight undeniable. "What's the point of knowing if we're too afraid to teach?" Her conviction was real, but Max could hear the underlying fear—the fear that they could make the wrong decision and doom the very legacy they sought to protect.

Max's fingers tightened around the compass, the metal warm against his palm, grounding him. He could feel the internal struggle gnawing at him, tearing him in two directions. On one hand, the thought of the scrolls being used for selfish or harmful purposes was horrifying. He pictured governments and corporations, hungry for power, seizing on the druids' wisdom to reshape the world in their

image. But on the other hand, the idea of locking this knowledge away, of letting it die with them, was equally unbearable. It was the same knowledge that had connected people to the earth, to the stars, to forces older than time itself. To keep that hidden felt like extinguishing a light that the world desperately needed. And now there was the compass—an object that seemed to know more than they did, as though its purpose was yet to fully reveal itself.

"There is a third option," Grandpa Ben said, his voice softer now, as if the weight of the moment was pressing down on him too. "We could pass the knowledge on—selectively. Teach only those who are ready. Those we can trust to use it with care and respect. It would take patience, caution, and discernment. We'd have to be careful with every step, but it might be the best way to honour the druids while ensuring their legacy isn't lost or misused."

Max's eyes drifted toward the towering stones around them. Their ancient presence felt both comforting and ominous, as if they too were waiting for the choice to be made. A gust of wind passed through the monument, rustling the grass at their feet, tugging at his hair. The stones seemed to whisper as the wind brushed against their surfaces—echoes of the past, of decisions made long ago. He felt the weight of the past pressing on him, not just from the druids but from the countless generations that had come before, each with their own battles and burdens. This decision wasn't just about them—it was about shaping the future, and the thought terrified him.

Lottie's voice pulled him back to the present. "What do you think, Max?" she asked, her eyes wide, searching his face for answers. "You've led us this far... What should we do?"

Max's heart pounded in his chest, each beat echoing in his ears like the slow, deliberate ticking of a clock. The compass in his pocket felt like a living thing now, its warmth almost burning against his skin, urging him to act. But how could he? Every choice felt impossible. If he chose wrong, the consequences could be devastating. A knot of doubt twisted in his gut, tightening with every second. What if I'm not the right person for this?

What if I fail?

He took a deep breath, the crisp morning air filling his lungs, grounding him. The sunlight bathed his face in warmth, and for a moment, he closed his eyes, letting the sensation wash over him. The compass pulsed again, steady, reassuring. Slowly, he opened his eyes and looked at Lottie, then at Grandpa Ben.

"I think," Max began, his voice stronger than he expected, "that we need to find a balance. The druids believed in balance—between nature, magic, and wisdom. We can't keep this hidden forever, but we also can't let it fall into the wrong hands. We need to teach it carefully, to the right people, those who will honour the legacy."

Grandpa Ben smiled—a small, proud smile, tinged with relief. "Wise words, Max. The druids would have agreed with you. They knew that knowledge, like power, must be used wisely and with great care."

Lottie nodded, her expression resolute now, though her arms remained crossed. "And we'll do it together, right? We'll protect the legacy, but we'll share it with those who deserve it."

Max smiled at his sister, feeling a sense of relief wash over him. "Yes, Lottie. Together. We've come this far, and we'll keep going. We'll make sure the druids' wisdom is used for good."

Grandpa Ben carefully closed the box of scrolls, the ancient knowledge locked away once more. But this time, it didn't feel like an ending. It felt like a beginning. The choice had been made—a choice that honoured the past while looking to the future with hope.

As they stood in the centre of Stonehenge, the first rays of sunlight spilled fully over the horizon, bathing the stones in golden light. The world around them seemed to hum with energy, the ancient magic woven into the stones themselves stirring to life. Max felt the compass warm again in his pocket, its glow a quiet promise. They had made their choice, but their journey was far from over.

Max looked toward the distant hills, his heart both heavy and light. Unseen forces lingered in the shadows, waiting for their next move, but Max knew they were ready. They had each other. They had the compass. And they had the wisdom of

the druids to guide them.

But something tugged at Max's thoughts, a quiet whisper in the back of his mind. Despite everything they had uncovered, he knew there were secrets still hidden within the compass itself—secrets that he hadn't yet unlocked. He could feel its pulse, steady but insistent, as though it was urging him to look deeper, to understand more. There was more to the druids' legacy than just these scrolls. What had the druids hidden away that they hadn't yet found? What mysteries did the compass still hold?

He glanced at Lottie and Grandpa Ben, knowing that they felt the weight of those same unanswered questions. Max silently vowed to himself that this wasn't the end—not of the druids' secrets, nor of their journey. He would pursue this further. He would speak with Lottie and Grandpa Ben, and together they would decide the best way forward. The compass had guided them this far, but its journey wasn't complete.

Together, they turned away from the ancient stones, the druids' legacy resting not just on their shoulders, but in their hearts—carried forward into the unknown.

Chapter 11: The Return Home

The train rumbled quietly along the tracks, the rhythmic clatter of wheels a soothing counterpoint to the whirlwind of thoughts racing through Max's mind. Beside him, Lottie rested her head against the window, her breath fogging the glass as she gazed out at the passing countryside. The fields and hills looked serene in the morning light, their green and gold hues a sharp contrast to the ancient, otherworldly atmosphere of Stonehenge. Across from them, Grandpa Ben sat with his arms crossed, eyes closed, though Max doubted he was actually sleeping.

They had all boarded the train back from their adventure earlier that morning,

slipping into the quiet hum of the commuter crowd. The return journey felt surreal, almost as if the world outside hadn't changed, even though everything inside Max had.

His fingers traced the smooth surface of the compass, now safely tucked in his pocket. It seemed to pulse faintly, reminding him of the weight it carried—of the secrets it had revealed and the responsibilities it had handed to them. A small, magical object, and yet it held so much power, so much history. And now, it was their burden to bear.

Lottie broke the silence, her voice soft but carrying a note of disbelief. "Do you think anyone will believe us if we tell them?"

Max glanced at her, catching the half-smile on her lips. "We can't tell them everything," he replied, his voice equally low, as though sharing a secret even though no one around could hear. "They wouldn't understand."

"I know," Lottie murmured, resting her head back against the seat. "But it's strange, isn't it? To have been through something so incredible and not be able to talk about it."

Max could only nod. He thought of their friends back at school, waiting for their return. They'd probably expect stories of a boring holiday, maybe some sight-seeing or visits to tourist spots. But how could he explain the enormity of what had actually happened? That they had ventured into ancient mysteries, confronted challenges that no one else had faced in centuries, and come out the other side with a responsibility that weighed on him more with each passing minute.

Grandpa Ben opened his eyes, giving them a knowing look. "Some things aren't meant to be shared yet," he said quietly, his voice carrying the wisdom of years. "The world isn't ready for what you've discovered. In time, maybe, but for now, it's our secret."

Max leaned back against the train seat, feeling the gentle vibration of the journey under him. The green sign for Elk Bank flashed past the window, signaling their approach to the nearest station. The familiar countryside surrounding Ross-

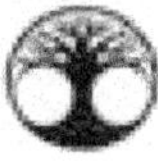

lyn appeared as they neared, but Max felt uneasy. They were returning, yes, but they were no longer the same.

The train slowed, then pulled into the station with a practiced halt. They gathered their bags and stepped onto the platform, the crisp morning air greeting them with a bite. The streets were quiet as they began the five-mile walk back to Rosslyn, each step a reminder that, while everything looked familiar, nothing felt the same anymore.

It wasn't a difficult walk; the rolling hills and lanes that had always been part of their lives now seemed more vivid, as though tinged with the magic they had uncovered. The compass remained in Max's pocket, pulsing lightly as they neared home, as if it, too, could sense the weight of their journey.

Chapter 12: The Disturbance

When they arrived back at Grandpa Ben's cottage, the first thing they noticed was the door. It was open—just a crack, but enough to send a chill down Max's spine.

"Did... did anyone leave the door open when we left?" Lottie whispered, her eyes wide with unease.

"No," Grandpa Ben said firmly, his voice low. "No one left it open."

Max's pulse quickened as the three of them stood on the threshold, staring into the dimly lit interior. The familiar scent of herbs and old books drifted toward them, but it did nothing to ease the tension that had settled over them. Everything looked the same as when they had left, yet it felt different—like the air itself had been disturbed.

"Someone's been here," Max muttered, his hand instinctively reaching for the compass in his pocket. The small object felt warm against his palm, almost as if it were warning him.

They hurried inside, their eyes scanning every corner. Nothing appeared out of place—the worn furniture was still where it had always been, and the clutter of books and papers scattered across the table hadn't been touched. But something was wrong. The silence in the house felt too thick, too heavy.

"Search the drawers," Grandpa Ben ordered, his voice hushed but urgent. Max and Lottie darted through the rooms, pulling open drawers and cabinets. Max's heart raced as they searched through old maps, notebooks, and the odd knick-knacks Grandpa Ben had collected over the years. But there was nothing missing. Nothing of value had been taken.

"Nothing's gone," Lottie said, breathless from their frantic search. "But someone was definitely here."

Grandpa Ben's brow furrowed, his eyes dark with thought. "They weren't looking for money or things," he said quietly. "They were looking for something else."

"The compass," Max whispered, his grip tightening on it. "But we had it with us the whole time."

"They know about it," Grandpa Ben said grimly, his voice hardening. "And now they know we have it. But they'll want more than just the compass."

Max felt a cold knot of dread form in his stomach. "The scrolls," he said, his voice barely audible. "We can't leave them here. It's too dangerous."

Lottie glanced around, her eyes wide. "Where can we hide them? If someone's watching us, they'll come back."

Grandpa Ben nodded. "We need a place where no one would think to look. Something clever, something that isn't obvious."

Max racked his brain, thinking through every possible option. The attic was too easy, and anything inside the house could be found if they were searched again. Then, an idea struck him.

"What about under the chapel?" Max asked suddenly. "There's a crypt down there, isn't there? No one would think to look beneath the village's chapel, and

it's close enough that we could get to it quickly if we need to."

Grandpa Ben's eyes lit up. "That could work," he said thoughtfully. "The chapel's crypt is old, and no one goes down there anymore. It would be perfect."

Lottie nodded in agreement. "We can hide them in a stone recess or one of the old tombs. No one would ever expect something so valuable to be kept in a place like that."

Grandpa Ben rubbed his chin, his expression serious. "It'll be dangerous, moving them. We'll need to do it at night, under cover of darkness, when we know no one's watching."

Max felt the tension lift slightly. They had a plan, and for now, it was the best option they had. But he couldn't shake the feeling that the danger was growing. Whoever had been watching them knew more than they let on—and the next time, they might not be so lucky.

The night air pressed in around them as they sat together in silence, the flickering light from the fireplace casting long shadows on the walls. They knew their journey was far from over, and that their enemies were growing closer. The scrolls were only the beginning, and now they had to protect not just the knowledge they'd uncovered, but themselves.

Chapter 13: The Hiding Place

Even though exhaustion weighed heavily on them, they knew there was no time to rest. Whoever had been watching them might return, and the scrolls—and the compass—needed to be hidden as soon as possible. The cottage felt too vulnerable, too exposed. They had to act quickly, and they had to be smart.

"We'll need torches," Grandpa Ben said, his voice firm but quiet, as though he didn't want to alert anyone who might be listening. "And dark clothes. We can't risk being spotted."

Max and Lottie exchanged a glance, a ripple of nervous energy passing between them. This wasn't just an adventure anymore—it was real, and the stakes were higher than ever. They rushed upstairs, pulling on dark sweaters and trousers, trying to stay as silent as possible. The house creaked with every step, the old wooden floorboards groaning beneath their feet, adding to the tension that hung in the air.

"Do you think they're still watching?" Lottie whispered as she tugged her hair into a tight ponytail.

Max paused, pulling a black hoodie over his head, and glanced out the window. The night outside was thick and impenetrable, the wind whistling through the trees in eerie gusts. He couldn't see anything unusual, but the feeling of being watched hadn't left him. "I don't know," he admitted. "But we can't take any chances."

They met Grandpa Ben downstairs, where he had already gathered their supplies: a small pack for the scrolls, torches, and an old leather pouch for the compass. His eyes were sharp and focused, and the usual warmth that Max was used to seeing in his grandfather had been replaced by the cool calculation of a man who had faced danger before.

"We'll head to the chapel," Grandpa Ben said in a low voice. "Move quietly and keep to the shadows. If anyone's out there, we don't want to draw attention."

Max and Lottie nodded, their hearts pounding as they pulled on their jackets and slung their bags over their shoulders. The reality of what they were about to do settled over them like a weight. They weren't just hiding relics—they were protecting something ancient, something that others would stop at nothing to find.

As they stepped out into the cold night, the darkness seemed to close in around them. The moon was hidden behind thick clouds, casting the village of Rosslyn into shadow. The path to the chapel was narrow and overgrown, winding through the woods that bordered their home. The wind rustled the leaves, and every snap of a twig or distant rustle made Max jump, his senses on high alert.

They moved quickly, their torches flickering like fireflies in the night, casting long

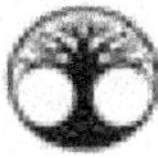

shadows on the trees that loomed above them. Lottie walked beside him, her movements cautious but steady. Max could see the tension in her eyes, but her determination hadn't wavered.

When they reached the chapel, it was even more imposing in the dark. The ancient stone walls seemed to hum with power, as though the secrets hidden within had awakened in anticipation of their arrival. Max shivered, not from the cold, but from the feeling that the chapel was more alive now than ever before.

Grandpa Ben led the way, his torch beam sweeping across the ground as he guided them to the old crypt. The door to the crypt was ancient, its heavy iron hinges rusted from centuries of exposure. With a grunt, Grandpa Ben pushed it open, the door creaking in protest, revealing a narrow staircase that spiraled down into the darkness.

Max swallowed hard, his heart racing as they descended into the crypt. The air grew colder, and the scent of damp stone filled his lungs. It felt as though they were stepping into a different world—one untouched by time.

"This should do," Grandpa Ben whispered as they reached the bottom of the stairs. The crypt was silent, save for the distant drip of water echoing off the stone walls. Tombs lined the narrow corridor, their ancient carvings barely visible in the dim light of their torches.

They moved to a corner, where one of the tombs had a small, hidden recess beneath it—a space just large enough for the scrolls and the compass. Max helped Grandpa Ben carefully place the scrolls inside, wrapping them in cloth to protect them from the damp. Lottie stood watch, her eyes darting nervously around the crypt, every creak and echo sending her heart racing.

Once the scrolls were secure, Grandpa Ben placed the compass inside the leather pouch and tucked it into the recess beside the scrolls. He paused for a moment, his hand resting on the cold stone, as if he were silently praying or asking for the chapel's protection.

"We've done all we can," Grandpa Ben said softly, his voice thick with emotion. "This is the safest place for now. But we'll need to stay vigilant. This is just the

beginning."

Max nodded, feeling the weight of the moment pressing down on him. He knew that their journey wasn't over—not by a long shot. But for now, at least, they had done what they needed to do.

As they made their way back up the stairs, the air around them seemed lighter, as though the chapel itself was watching over their secret. But Max couldn't shake the feeling that they weren't alone—that somewhere in the shadows, someone was waiting for their next move

Chapter 14: Epilogue - The Adventure Continues

The days following their return from Stonehenge were filled with a strange calm. Max, Lottie, and Grandpa Ben had come to a quiet but firm decision: the scrolls and the compass were too powerful to be left out in the open. They had placed them in the hidden recess beneath the village chapel, locked away from prying eyes. For now, they agreed, they would leave them there, untouched, for a few days—time to let things settle, to recover from the whirlwind of their recent journey.

But even with the scrolls and compass out of sight, their presence loomed large in their minds. Every evening, as the sun dipped below the horizon and the stars twinkled in the night sky, the three of them would gather around the old wooden table in Grandpa Ben's cottage. The cottage was the same, yet the air felt different—thicker, heavier, as if the weight of their discovery had seeped into the walls.

Max found himself lost in thought more often than not, replaying the events of Stonehenge in his mind. There were moments when he could almost feel the pulse of the ancient magic they had uncovered, as though the power beneath the earth still called out to him. The thrill of the adventure had faded, replaced by the sobering realization that they were now the keepers of something much bigger than themselves.

Lottie, too, had grown quieter, more reflective. Max often caught her gazing out the window, her brow furrowed in thought. She wasn't the same carefree girl who had bounded into every challenge headfirst. Something had changed in her, in all of them. They had stepped into a world of ancient responsibility, and now that they were back, the everyday routine of life felt distant—almost irrelevant.

One evening, Max found himself staring at the compass, still feeling the warmth of its glow in his mind. Even though it was hidden away beneath the chapel, he could sense its power, as if it were reaching out to him across the village. The decision to leave it and the scrolls undisturbed had been the right one—at least for now—but he knew it wouldn't be long before the compass called to them again.

As he sat there, Grandpa Ben spoke, his voice thoughtful. "We've done the right thing, giving ourselves time to rest. But don't mistake this quiet for an ending. The druids' legacy is far from finished with us."

Max nodded, though his heart felt heavy. "Do you think we're really ready for what's coming?" he asked softly, the doubt creeping back into his voice.

Grandpa Ben's eyes were steady as he regarded Max. "No one's ever truly ready for something like this. But the compass chose you for a reason. It'll guide you when the time is right."

Lottie, sitting across from them, broke her silence. "We'll face it together, right?" Her voice was firm, but there was a trace of uncertainty in her eyes—one Max hadn't noticed before.

Max looked at her, understanding her hesitation. They had changed—more than they'd realized. "Yeah, together," he said, though part of him still wondered if they could ever really be prepared for what lay ahead.

In the days that followed, they avoided talking about the scrolls or the compass. They returned to school, tried to slip back into their old routines, but it wasn't easy. Max found it hard to concentrate in class, his thoughts always drifting back to the crypt, to the scrolls they had left behind. Every time he passed the chapel, he felt a strange pull, as though the earth itself was trying to draw him back to the hidden knowledge they had discovered.

At night, he would lie awake, staring at the ceiling, wondering what the scrolls truly meant—what the balance they spoke of really was. The more he thought about it, the more the world around him seemed fragile, like everything was balanced on a razor's edge. Was it really their responsibility to protect it?

One evening, several days after they had hidden the scrolls, Max could stand it no longer. He returned to the table, pulling out his notebook where he had sketched some of the symbols they had uncovered. He had barely touched the page when a familiar warmth spread through him—a feeling that stopped him in his tracks.

The compass. Even from its hiding place beneath the chapel, he could sense it calling to him.

"Grandpa," Max said quietly, looking up from his notebook. "It's happening again. I can feel it. The compass… it's pointing somewhere new."

Grandpa Ben looked up from his chair, his face serious. He didn't need to ask what Max meant. The compass had chosen them once more. "Then we're not done yet," he said, his voice grave. "But be careful, Max. The deeper you go, the more dangerous it will become."

Lottie stepped forward, her earlier hesitation replaced by a fierce determination. "We've come this far," she said. "We're ready."

The days following their return from Stonehenge were a strange blend of quiet reflection and the bubbling excitement of hidden knowledge. After much thought, they had decided not to leave the scrolls and compass beneath the chapel. Instead, Grandpa Ben had revealed a hidden panel he had built into the floor of the cottage—a safe and secret compartment where they could keep the relics closer, protected from prying eyes.

With the scrolls and the compass now securely stored beneath their feet, they began to decipher the ancient writings. Every evening, as the sky darkened and the stars twinkled overhead, Max, Lottie, and Grandpa Ben gathered around the wooden table. The hidden compartment was opened, and the scrolls unrolled, their ancient symbols flickering in the glow of the lantern.

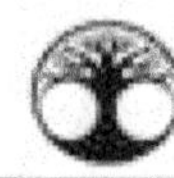

Max had never felt so absorbed in anything before. Each scroll revealed more about the druids, about their understanding of balance and the delicate threads that connected all living things. As they read, Max could feel the weight of the responsibility growing. This wasn't just a treasure hunt or a thrilling adventure. This was real—something far larger than themselves.

One evening, Max found himself staring at the newest scroll they had unrolled. It was different from the others, the symbols more intricate, more foreboding. As his fingers traced the markings, something inside him stirred. A strange sensation fluttered in his chest—part fear, part anticipation. The scroll seemed to pulse under his fingertips, alive with ancient power. He felt the weight of it pressing down on him, a quiet, invisible force that seemed to breathe in the air around him.

His eyes locked onto a passage, one that spoke of a protector—someone chosen to safeguard the balance of the world. The words felt personal, as if they had been written just for him. He read the line again: ***The protector bears the weight of many worlds, but it is the heart that guides him.***

Max's breath caught in his throat. His fingers trembled as they followed the text, his mind racing. Was he this protector? His heart pounded against his ribs. He wasn't ready for this—not even close. He was just Max, a kid with too many questions and too few answers. Yet, deep down, something shifted. He felt a strange, undeniable pull toward the words, like the prophecy had been waiting for him all along. He looked up at Grandpa Ben, whose eyes met his with quiet understanding. There was no need for words between them. This was more than just an adventure. It was a responsibility—his responsibility. Whatever lay ahead, it would be up to him to face it.

The Compass Glows

Just as Max began to roll up the scroll, the compass in his pocket grew warm again. Slowly, almost reluctantly, he pulled it out. The needle spun wildly before settling—not pointing north, but deep into the forest beyond the village. The faint

glow it gave off cast eerie shadows on the cottage walls, dancing in rhythm with Max's pounding heart.

"Grandpa," Max said, his voice low, a knot forming in his stomach, "it's happening again. The compass—it's pointing somewhere new."

Grandpa Ben's eyes narrowed as he looked at the glowing compass. His expression was a mix of pride and caution. "The druids' secrets are not yet fully revealed," he said thoughtfully. "The compass has chosen you, Max, to uncover what lies ahead. But be careful—the deeper you go, the more dangerous it may become."

Lottie leaned forward, her earlier hesitation replaced with steely determination. The uncertainty that had lingered in her voice since Stonehenge was gone, replaced with a fierceness Max recognized all too well. "We'll face it together," she said firmly. "We're ready."

Max wasn't sure if *he* was ready. But as he held the glowing compass in his hand, he knew one thing for certain—this was only the beginning.

Ian McEwan: Problem Solver, Author, and Creative Explorer

Ian McEwan is a multifaceted individual with a deep passion for both creative storytelling and practical problem-solving. With over 30 years of experience in the offshore industry, Ian has built an impressive career as a project planner and scheduler. His work has taken him around the world, including a significant stint in Africa.

Yet, beyond the technical world, Ian has a rich creative side. He is a self-taught digital artist with a thirst for knowledge, further developing his skills through platforms like LinkedIn Learning. Recently, Ian has embraced the possibilities of artificial intelligence, using it as a tool in both his professional and personal endeavours. He even authored a children's book on how to get the best out of ChatGPT, sharing his knowledge of technology in a fun, approachable way.

Ian's creativity also shines through in his writing. He is currently working on multiple writing projects, including a compelling story titled The Compass of the Moon and Stars. The narrative follows Max, Lottie, and their grandfather, Grandpa Ben, on a magical journey tied to ancient druids and the mysteries of Stonehenge. Ian masterfully blends elements of fantasy, mystery, and adventure, and he is also planning a sequel set in Scotland, where his characters will follow the compass to Dunadd Fort. The sequel will unfold in nine chapters, taking place in the seafaring town of Oban.

Ian's creative spirit and technical expertise make him a unique individual, one who blends a sharp, analytical mind with a vivid imagination. Whether he's solving logistical challenges, crafting compelling stories, or exploring new technologies, Ian approaches every challenge with curiosity, determination, and a deep sense of purpose. He's not only a problem solver but a storyteller, a creator, and a trailblazer in both his professional and personal life.

The Compass of the Moon and Stars

Max and Lottie have always found solace in their quiet village of Rosslyn, with its ancient chapel and mysterious forests. But after a tragic accident that leaves them in the care of their grandfather, their lives take a thrilling turn. When a mysterious compass with magical properties is delivered to them, it sets off a chain of events that will lead them to the ancient monument of Stonehenge.

Guided by their wise and enigmatic Grandpa Ben, Max and Lottie soon discover that the compass is connected to the ancient druids and a powerful secret hidden for centuries. As they journey deeper into the mysteries of Stonehenge, they encounter ancient trials, cryptic scrolls, and the hidden Order of the Hidden Compass—an ancient group sworn to protect the wisdom of the druids.

In a race against time, Max and Lottie must unravel the secrets of the stars and nature, while confronting their own fears and doubts. Together, they must decide how to protect the powerful knowledge they uncover, knowing that forces from the past are watching—and waiting to seize control.

The Compass of the Moon and Stars is a magical adventure that blends ancient history with thrilling discovery, as two siblings uncover the power of courage, knowledge, and the ties that bind us to the past.